"*I intend to get a job in London.*"

"And leave Ben here?"

That suggestion was so outrageous that she was forced to lift her head. "Of course not," she said. "Ben lives with me." She swallowed. "I can only assume you're joking. Well, let me tell you, it was in very bad—"

"I wasn't joking." Alex's voice was flat. "I think it's an eminently suitable arrangement. He's lived with you for the past four years. I think it's time he lived with his father."

Sara's jaw dropped. "I beg your—?" She gathered her scattered senses. "Ben's father is dead."

"Is he?" There was a depressing note of conviction in his words. "We both know Harry wasn't Ben's father, so why don't we stop pretending?"

ANNE MATHER began writing when she was a child, progressing through torrid teenage romances to the kind of adult romances she likes to read now. She's married, and lives in the north of England. After writing, she enjoys reading, driving and traveling to different places to find settings for new novels. She considers herself very lucky to do something that she not only enjoys, but also gets paid for.

Books by Anne Mather

HARLEQUIN PRESENTS
1697—STRANGE INTIMACY
1722—BRITTLE BONDAGE
1731—RAW SILK
1759—TREACHEROUS LONGINGS
1797—A WOMAN OF PASSION

Don't miss any of our special offers. Write to us at the following address for information on our newest releases.

Harlequin Reader Service
U.S.: 3010 Walden Ave., P.O. Box 1325, Buffalo, NY 14269
Canadian: P.O. Box 609, Fort Erie, Ont. L2A 5X3

Anne Mather

Relative Sins

Harlequin Books

**TORONTO • NEW YORK • LONDON
AMSTERDAM • PARIS • SYDNEY • HAMBURG
STOCKHOLM • ATHENS • TOKYO • MILAN
MADRID • WARSAW • BUDAPEST • AUCKLAND**

ISBN 0-373-11845-7

RELATIVE SINS

First North American Publication 1996.

Copyright © 1996 by Anne Mather.

This edition published by arrangement with Harlequin Books S.A.

® and TM are trademarks of the publisher. Trademarks indicated with
® are registered in the United States Patent and Trademark Office, the
Canadian Trade Marks Office and in other countries.

Printed in U.S.A.

CHAPTER ONE

'I AM the resurrection, and the life, said the Lord...'

The minister's voice went on, the strangely familiar words of the funeral service arousing disbelief as well as numbing grief. The November day was icy, and the crowd gathered about the grave huddled deeper into their dark coats and warm gloves. Sara was fairly sure that they were wishing it were over, not just because of the unhappy circumstances, but because it reminded them of how truly mortal man was.

For herself, she had the feeling that she'd never be warm again. The chill she was experiencing came from inside as well as out. Her feet were freezing and her hands were cold, but she was hardly aware of physical discomfort. It was her emotions that felt as if they were encased in ice.

Thankfully, the ritual was almost over. In a little while she could escape so many sympathetic eyes and grieve in peace. One or two of those in attendance had raised handkerchiefs to their faces, quietly dabbing at their eyes or blowing noses to disguise an errant tear.

Harry's mother was one of them, and Sara wished that she could feel closer to her mother-in-law. But Elizabeth Reed had never shown any affection for her daughter-in-law while Harry had been alive, and Sara suspected that she blamed her now for Harry's untimely death.

The little boy standing beside Sara tugged at her sleeve, and she turned at once at the distraction. 'Stand still, darling,' she whispered softly. 'We'll be leaving soon.'

And then she immediately felt a pang of disloyalty for saying the words. All the same, if it hadn't been for Elizabeth Reed Ben would not have attended his father's funeral, and Sara was still of the opinion that her son was far too young to share their grief.

'But I'm cold,' Ben persisted, and scuffed his toe at a clod of earth.

'I suppose we all are,' Sara replied comfortingly. 'But, I've told you, it won't be long now. At least it isn't raining.' That would have been the final straw.

Ben's dark head turned to look at the row of cars parked outside the churchyard. Watching him, Sara realised that her four-year-old son hadn't comprehended the seriousness of the occasion. She'd told him that his father had gone to heaven, that he wouldn't be coming back again. But she was sure he imagined heaven was some distant corner of his universe, and that in a while they'd all go home.

But where was home? she wondered unhappily, aware that Elizabeth Reed was watching them, and no doubt deploring Ben's lack of discretion. Certainly not in Brazil, where Harry had died, and definitely not at Perry Edmunds, where her in-laws had always lived.

Tears came, unbidden, to Sara's eyes and she tried to blink them away. She'd tried not show her grief too openly for Ben's sake, but now and then the realisation overwhelmed her.

How could the urban guerillas whom Harry had so often negotiated with and trusted have mistaken him for a political opponent? The ambush, on a remote and mountainous section of the highway, had put Harry in the wrong place at the wrong time. The attempted assassination of the diplomat whom Harry had been accompanying had gone tragically wrong, and her husband had not expected to die at the hands of people he had previously befriended.

A bullet from one of the guerillas' illegally obtained rifles had hit Harry in the neck, and although he had been rushed to a hospital in São Joaquim it had been too late. His life had proved to be just another trophy in the increasing war that was raging between affluence and poverty, power and subjugation in the world today. Ironically, Harry had been working to break down the very divides in the country's class system he had died for. When they had brought the news to Sara in Rio she had felt his frustration above all else...

'Will we be going home in that long black car?'

Ben's question relieved the sense of anguish she was feeling, and she realised that she owed it to Harry's memory to give her son all the love he deserved. It wasn't his fault that his father was dead, nor hers—only Harry's mother found that hard to accept. But she had to acknowledge that that part of her life was over, and she and Ben were on their own now against the world.

'I expect so,' she answered him gently, and as she returned her eyes to the coffin it was lowered majestically into the ground. It was left to her to make one final gesture, and, plucking a peach-coloured rose from a wreath, she tossed it swiftly into the grave.

The vicar gave his final blessing and gradually the mourners began to drift away. Some of them—the Reverend Mr Bowden amongst them—approached Sara, and, clasping her hand, offered their sincere condolences. Others, she knew, she would see back at the house—not least the staff at Perry Edmunds, who had loved Harry as their own.

She wondered if any of them found it as difficult to equate the humorous man she had known and loved with the gloomy service in the churchyard. It was hard to imagine leaving Harry here, and she had to remind herself that it was only his body, not his spirit, in the grave. In spirit Harry would always inhabit the warmer places of the world—the villa they had lived in in Kuwait, perhaps, or the sprawling bungalow in Rio.

'Sara.'

She stiffened.

She'd been expecting to hear that voice ever since she and Ben had arrived in England. She'd actually been half-afraid that he might come to meet her at the airport. After all, she'd reasoned, he was bound to have flown home for his brother's funeral. Harry had been the only sibling he had.

But only Harry's father had been waiting in the arrivals hall. And when they'd arrived at the house only Elizabeth Reed had been there. She hadn't learned until the following morning that Alex was on a filming assignment in Kashmir, and that so far they had not been able to reach him.

'I'm sorry.' Alex spoke again, but whether he was apologising for being late or offering his condolences for Harry's death she couldn't be sure. She didn't particularly care, she thought rather bitterly. It would have been so much easier for her if he'd stayed away.

'I know you must be thinking the worst, but I did get here as fast as I could. Unfortunately I didn't get into London until after midnight, and I couldn't get a connecting flight until this morning.'

His explanation was legitimate enough, and Sara had no doubt that he had come as quickly as he'd been able. Bearing in mind his busy schedule, she amended uncharitably. Alex always had lived life to the full.

'It doesn't matter,' she replied now, her expression revealing nothing of the turmoil she felt inside. He'd be gone again in a couple of days, she reassured herself tensely. Until then, surely she could be polite.

'We'll talk at the house,' Alex added, and she was forced to meet his piercing eyes. 'Just remember—I'm here if you need me. It's what Harry would have wanted, I know.'

Do you? she thought.

For a moment Sara felt a wave of almost crippling fury sweep over her, and her anger demanded some kind of outlet for its force. But Harry's parents had joined them, Elizabeth taking Ben's hand and leading him away, turning them into a family unit which she had no right to break—well, not at this moment anyway, Sara thought grimly. Later they would see. She didn't need anyone's help, particularly not Alex Reed's.

To her relief he seemed to sense that this was not the time to put pressure on her, and although she resented it he accompanied his mother to the car. Watching him talking to Ben in that charming way he had, introducing himself to her son and making him smile, irritated her beyond belief. He had no right to do that, she thought indignantly. Harry's son meant nothing to him.

'Come along.'

Harry's father touched her arm, and she turned to look at Robert Reed with some remorse. This wasn't easy for any of them, and she had to keep her head until it was over.

'Don't think too badly of him,' murmured her father-in-law as they walked to where the limousines were waiting, and Sara had no difficulty in interpreting whom he meant. 'If Newcastle hadn't been fogbound, he'd have landed here before nine o'clock. As it was, the flight was diverted to Tees-side and he had to hire a car from there.'

'Well, it is a raw day,' Sara offered, realising that she couldn't expect his father to understand how she felt about her brother-in-law. And fortunately Robert didn't notice anything amiss.

'I imagine it's quite a change from the kind of climate you're used to,' he commented. And then, as if regret-

ting his implication, he went on, 'You must think of
Perry Edmunds as your home now.'

'Thank you.'

Sara managed the words of gratitude, but she knew
that she couldn't stay here. Apart from anything else she
had to get a job. She had no intention of living on the
Reeds' charity, and she doubted if Harry's pension would
support her. She had been working in London when
she'd met Harry, and that was where she expected to
make her home.

All the same, as she climbed into the back of the lim-
ousine beside Elizabeth and her son she couldn't help
thinking how swiftly things could change. Two weeks
ago the most important decision she'd had to make was
which wine to serve at dinner. Now her husband was
dead, her son was without a father, and the pleasant life
they'd had in Rio was just a bitter-sweet memory.

'Are you all right?'

Her mother-in-law was eyeing her intently now, and
Sara wondered what Elizabeth thought she'd seen in her
face—regret, perhaps, grief, sorrow certainly, but was
she looking for remorse, for a self-reproach that Sara
couldn't feel?

She knew that her mother-in-law blamed her for
Harry's taking his family to Brazil in the first place.
Working for the Foreign Office, he could no doubt have
requested a posting in London after Kuwait, but the
thought of coming back to England after two years spent
in the heat of a tropical climate had not appealed to
Harry, and it had been his decision to take his family to
Rio and prolong their tenure overseas.

'Besides,' he'd argued when Sara had felt obliged to
make a token plea on behalf of the Reeds, 'Ben will have
to go to school soon, and then we'll probably settle in
England for a while. Let's enjoy our freedom while we

have it. We'll have years and years of boredom when we get back.'

Sara's lips trembled, and she determinedly caught the lower one between her teeth and bit it. She didn't want anyone's sympathy. She'd handle this in her own way— well, she and Ben together, she thought tenderly. What would she do without her son?

Which prompted the realisation that sooner or later she was going to have to sit down with Ben and explain the situation to him. It was all very well consoling herself with the thought that none of this would really touch him. The fact remained that he had to be made to understand their new circumstances. They weren't going to have a lot of money, and Ben was going to find living in the small house or apartment that she would be able to afford for them vastly different from the luxurious bungalow that had been his home these last two years.

The sedate journey from St Matthew's, which lay on the outskirts of the village of Edmundsfield, to Perry Edmunds, the Reeds' house, only took a few minutes. Without the top-hatted figure of the chief mourner, striding along at the head of the procession of cars, the drivers quickened their pace. Probably as eager as she was, Sara thought ruefully, to leave the churchyard behind.

Was there ever such a contrast as between the heat and colour of South America and Northumberland in the depths of winter? Even the trees were stark and skeletal, the grass a dirty green beneath their feet.

Alex and his father were occupying the seats immediately behind the driver, and despite her best efforts Sara couldn't help but be aware that Alex was a bare two or three feet in front of her. She'd hoped that she'd never have to see him again, that he'd find the prospect of visiting his brother and his wife boring—and so far he had. And since Harry's death, she had to admit, she'd wished it had been him...

Ben stared out of the window for most of the journey, and Sara diverted herself by wondering what her son was thinking. Certainly their present surroundings were entirely unfamiliar to a little boy who was used to the overcrowded cities and forever stretching beaches of the southern hemisphere. Yet he hadn't complained, except for that moment by the graveside when he'd said he was cold. He'd been almost preternaturally obedient, and she could only assume that the gravity of the situation had got to him in some way at least.

She sighed. When they'd boarded the plane to London a few days ago—the plane which had, incidentally, brought his father's lifeless body home for burial—he had seemed to regard the whole trip as a kind of adventure. He'd been excited about coming to England— a place he didn't even know. He had been born in the army hospital in Kuwait, Sara remembered tightly. Had Harry sensed how desperate she'd been to get away...?

Now, however, they were back with a vengeance, with no obvious alternative in sight. She really would have to try and explain their situation to Ben. However difficult it might prove, she owed him that at least.

'You're very quiet,' remarked Elizabeth beside her, and Sara realised that Harry's mother was still waiting for her to say how she was.

'I'm tired,' she said, with an involuntary gesture of apology. 'I haven't slept very well since we got back.'

'At least you're alive,' remarked Elizabeth in an undertone. 'How lucky you weren't with Harry when he was killed.' The underlying message was clear, and Sara guessed that now that her husband had been buried his mother wouldn't hesitate to show her claws.

'Liz!'

Evidently Robert Reed had heard his wife's comment too, and to Sara's relief the older woman said no more. But Sara had no doubt that the subject had only been abandoned for the time being. Harry's mother would probably return to it when they were alone.

The car glided between the gates of Perry Edmunds, and Ben turned round to kneel on the seat. 'The other cars are following us!' he exclaimed. 'Are we going to have a party?' He drew back to look at his mother. 'Will Daddy be there?'

'Your father's dead, Ben!' exclaimed his grandmother tautly. She looked at Sara. 'I thought you'd told him. Where does he think we've been?'

'I don't imagine he associated this morning's events with anything, Mother,' declared Alex impatiently, glancing over his shoulder. 'I don't know why Sara thought he ought to attend. He's far too young.'

If Sara had hoped that Mrs Reed might explain that Ben's attendance had been her idea, she was disappointed. The cars had negotiated the curving drive and were stopping in the courtyard before the house, and Harry's mother thrust open her door and climbed out. Ben followed her before Sara could prevent him, and she was forced to watch her mother-in-law grasp his hand and lead him indoors.

'She's upset.'

Alex's unwelcome solicitude was almost more than she could take. 'Aren't we all?' she said, hoping Harry's father would forgive her, and, ignoring any assistance, she stepped out of the car.

Mrs Fraser, the Reeds' housekeeper, had evidently beaten them back from the church, and was standing at the door of the house now, awaiting the return of the family. She was a middle-aged Scottish woman, dour of appearance but gentle of manner, who had worked for Elizabeth Reed for the past twenty-five years.

Sensitive to the day's events, she offered Sara a compassionate smile. 'The little one's away for some lemonade,' she declared, referring to Ben's disappearance. 'I'll see that he takes no harm. He can eat his lunch with Alison and myself.'

'Thank you, Mrs Fraser.' Sara was grateful, as much to know that her son was not being manipulated by his grandmother as for the housekeeper's obvious kindness. 'I expect you'll find he's hungry. His appetite hasn't suffered, thank goodness.'

'Not like his mother's,' observed Mrs Fraser, with rather more outspokenness than was usual. Her lips curved down at her presumption but she didn't withdraw her statement. It made Sara feel that at least someone at Perry Edmunds cared about *her* welfare as well.

Once inside the house Sara wished that she could have a few minutes to herself, but the cars that had followed them back from the cemetery were disgorging their passengers, and everyone expected Harry's widow to be there to accept their condolences.

It didn't prevent the sense of isolation that enveloped her, however. Despite being surrounded by people, she had never felt more alone. Perhaps she should have kept Ben with her after all, she thought. At least he provided her with the confidence she lacked. But a child couldn't be expected to understand how she was feeling, and it wasn't fair to use him in that way.

Blinking back tears which she felt sure must look rather obvious, Sara endeavoured to regain her composure. After all, she'd made it this far; surely she could sustain herself for another couple of hours? This was almost the final ritual. All that was left was dealing with Harry's will.

She moved closer to the huge open fire that added warmth and light to the somewhat sombre atmosphere of the hall. For all Perry Edmunds was an imposing house from the outside, inside it was inclined to be gloomy, with dark oak panelling and lofty ceilings that never seemed to garner any heat. It had been built in the last century, and such modifications as had been made were mostly superficial. And although it was supposed to be centrally heated Sara hadn't felt really warm since she'd arrived from Brazil.

But that wasn't really so unusual, she reminded herself quickly. Apart from the circumstances of her return, this northernmost county of England was a far cry from the corner of Brazil that she and Harry had called home. Naturally she'd noticed the change of temperature—in the inhabitants as well as in the weather, she thought ruefully.

She was shedding her coat and the fine calfskin gloves that she had worn to the funeral when Mrs Fraser reappeared to check on the extra staff hired for the occasion. After ensuring that everyone had been supplied with either sherry or whisky—Sara noticed that most of the men had chosen the latter—the housekeeper stopped beside Sara and assured her that Ben was quite settled in the kitchen.

'He's having lemonade and shortbread,' she said. 'I made the shortbread myself this morning. Now, just you take things easy. We don't want you falling ill now, do we?'

'I couldn't agree more.'

A tall shadow fell across them, and Sara had no need to turn her head to identify the intruder. Where Alex was concerned she was discovering that she had a sixth sense. She would have liked to walk away, but politeness dictated otherwise.

'I'm perfectly all right,' she said, her words addressed to no one in particular, but she was aware that Alex and Mrs Fraser exchanged a speaking look. Dammit, she thought, she wasn't a child; she didn't need anyone to fuss over her. And as for asking Alex for help... Well, actions spoke louder than words.

'I'd better go and see how Alison's getting on with the salmon,' declared Mrs Fraser, evidently deciding that her presence was no longer needed. 'You can tell your mother the buffet is ready, whenever she decides she wants it serving,' she added to Alex. 'I just hope there'll be enough.' She glanced around the thickening crowd in the hall and grimaced. 'I'm sure Mr Reed just told me to cater for eighty, but it looks like there's over a hundred here already.'

A *hundred*?

Sara glanced about her, realising that many of the people who had thronged St Matthew's church had come to pay their respects. Because only some of them had gathered at Harry's graveside she had imagined that they were the only mourners, but now she realised how mistaken she'd been.

She realised also that one of the reasons why Alex had positioned himself at her side was that eventually they would all drift in her direction. At present Harry's mother and father were doing the honours, but Sara couldn't expect to remain aloof for much longer.

All the same, she did not need *his* support...

'It'll soon be over.'

His words irritated her for no good reason, and she tilted her head to give him a studied look. 'For which I'm sure you'll be very grateful,' she remarked, aware that she was being ungracious. 'Tell me, is this one of your flying visits, or can your parents expect you to stay for forty-eight hours this time?'

Alex's lips thinned. 'I shan't be going back to Kashmir,' he said obliquely. And then, as one of his father's tenants came to offer his condolences, he added, 'I don't think you know Will Baxter, Sara. He and his son run a small printing works in Corbridge.'

For the next few minutes Sara was obliged to shelve any alarm that Alex's words might have engendered and accept the sympathy offered by a sequence of well-meaning strangers. So many people came to take her hand and offer some personal glimpse of the man who had been her husband that she lost track of names and faces.

But these were Harry's friends, Harry relations—aunts and uncles and cousins whom Sara had never even met. She had got to know Harry in London, and had visited Edmundsfield only a couple of times before they were married. Harry had told her little about his life here— a fact which her mother-in-law had soon discovered. She was a stranger to these people, just as they were strangers to her.

Perhaps if they'd been married here... she found herself thinking now, and then dismissed the thought before it was fully formed. There was no way that she could have been married in Edmundsfield. For all her brief acquaintance, this village held only unhappy memories for her.

'And I don't live here,' Alex was informing her evenly, and she realised that once again they were alone. Or as alone as any two people could be in such a gathering, she amended silently. But at least his words reassured her. He'd be going back to London if not to Kashmir.

'I really think I ought to go and check on my son,' she declared, avoiding any direct answer as he had himself. 'If you'll excuse me...'

'I bought Ragdale,' he said before she could put enough space between them so that she could pretend not to hear. 'I've left the Press Corps. I decided I needed some security in my old age.'

Sara swallowed, though the effort nearly choked her. 'How...interesting,' she said, obliged to say something before she rushed away. But the news was devastating, particularly as the Reeds were bound to want to see their grandson on a regular basis. God, hadn't fate dealt her enough blows already? Was she now to be expected to treat Alex like a friend? Like a *brother-in-law*, she thought scornfully. A man she'd grown to hate.

When she returned to the hall a few minutes later it was Robert Reed who captured her attention. 'We're about to have something to eat,' he said, 'and I don't want to hear that you're not hungry. There's scarcely anything of you as it is. Have you been starving yourself to stay slim?'

Sara managed a faint smile. 'I don't know whether that's a compliment or not,' she teased, relieved to find that she felt no sense of intimidation with him. Harry had been like his father, she thought: competent but easygoing, never letting anyone rile him, never losing his temper out of hand. Or his head, she appended somewhat painfully, wishing desperately that he were still here. He'd been her friend, her lover, her anchor—the only man she'd ever known who'd thought of others before himself...

CHAPTER TWO

DESPITE her best efforts, Sara could only manage to eat one sandwich and the crumbled remains of a piece of Mrs Fraser's shortbread. Even so, the sugary biscuit stuck in her throat, and she found herself drinking more than was wise to try and dislodge the constriction.

She knew that Harry's father was concerned about her, which warmed that part of her that his wife had so unfeelingly chilled. And at least Alex hadn't returned to disturb her, though the sight of him, chatting to a tall, elegant woman in her thirties, wasn't exactly to her taste either.

She'd recognised the woman earlier, when she and her husband had come to offer their condolences. The Erskines—and Linda Erskine in particular—were old friends of the family. At one time Linda Adams, as she had been then, had been expected to marry one of the brothers, but circumstances had decreed otherwise, and Harry's mother had informed them in one of her letters that she'd married James Erskine instead.

A great disappointment, no doubt, thought Sara now rather maliciously, remembering the way Linda had hung around Alex when she was here. It had seemed only a matter of time before their engagement was to be announced, and she knew that Harry had been surprised that his brother had ducked the issue. But then, Harry hadn't known what manner of man his brother was...

Sara pressed her lips together. She didn't want to think about any of that now—not here, not with Harry dead and Alex playing the grieving sibling. But how could he

19

behave so ingenuously, she wondered, as if Harry's death had devastated him as much as anyone else? He was the man who had betrayed his brother, yet he was acting as if they'd been the best of friends.

All the same, Sara's eyes lingered on Linda Erskine and her brother-in-law with something less than indifference. The woman's simple navy blue dress, worn with matching stockings and high-heeled shoes, served to enhance both a graceful neck and the silken ash-blonde hair that Linda wore in a fashionable chignon. There was a brooch at her shoulder which offered some relief from the rather severe outfit, but Sara thought, rather uncharitably, that its expensive setting was a reminder that Linda had married well.

From Sara's point of view the exquisite emeralds, set in a twisted coil of white gold, were an all too unwelcome reminder of the home she had once had. Beautiful gems like those were freely available in South America, and Harry had offered to buy her an emerald ring for their fifth wedding anniversary.

Sara determinedly put that thought aside and glanced instead at her own appearance in the mirror over the fireplace. The dress she had been forced to wear wasn't entirely suitable, being too thin for this northern climate. But it was plain and it was black, and she hadn't exactly had a lot of choice.

The long coat she had worn to the church was infinitely more suitable. She'd bought it in London years ago, and for some reason she'd taken it with her when she moved. Being made of warm charcoal-grey wool, it had hidden the fact that the dress hung rather loosely on her spare frame. She knew she'd lost weight since Harry's death, and she hadn't been exactly robust before that. Food had never been that important to her, and since Harry had been killed she'd found it difficult to eat anything.

In consequence she found her comparison to Linda Erskine decidedly unflattering. Despite the fact that her skin was lightly tanned and clear of any blemishes, she was sure that it suffered from a lack of colour. The other woman's make-up was smooth and immaculate, a distinctive touch of blusher heightening the impression of a perfect English rose.

Sara's hand crept almost unconsciously to her hair. Unlike Linda's, Sara's hair barely brushed her collar at the back. In the heat of Rio de Janeiro it had been more sensible to keep it short, and although its russet strands were thick and shining it lacked the elegance of a longer style. Perhaps now that she was back in England...

But at that point she arrested her thoughts. For heaven's sake, she thought impatiently, here she was, at Harry's *funeral*, and all she could think about was how dowdy she looked when compared with a woman she scarcely knew. What did it matter to her if she looked a frump? She wasn't here to gather compliments. She was here to bury her husband.

'Sara? It is Sara, isn't it?'

The voice at her shoulder was unfamiliar, and she turned almost guiltily to find Linda Erskine's husband hovering at her side. His appearance caused her to look with some apprehension across the hall, but Linda was still standing with Alex and seemed indifferent to anyone else.

'I—why, yes,' she said, forcing herself to concentrate on her companion and not speculate on his wife's behaviour. Though if she had been James Erskine she wouldn't have left them, she thought bitterly. Someone should warn him that people weren't always what they seemed.

'I should introduce myself,' he was saying now. 'I'm James Erskine. Harry's father and I have been friends for years. I was so sorry to hear what happened. Harry was a fine man and I admired him greatly. You have my sympathy at this most stressful time.'

'Thank you.' Sara wasn't sure whether she should address him as James or Mr Erskine, and as she was having some difficulty in separating him from the rather envious thoughts she had been having about his wife she decided to use neither.

'It must all be quite bewildering for you,' James went on, revealing a genuine compassion for her plight. 'Coming back to Edmundsfield must have been daunting. Not just another country, but a wintry one as well.'

'Yes.' Sara managed a faint smile. 'You forget how cold it can be. I'm afraid I've been spoilt for the past five years. I've forgotten what it feels like to wear an overcoat.'

James smiled in return. 'I, on the other hand, know what it feels like only too well. When you get to my age you have to take care of yourself. It wouldn't do for me to leave my overcoat behind.'

Sara warmed to him. His friendly smile, his obvious willingness to joke about his age, his understanding all commended him to her. When the news of his marriage to Linda had reached them Harry had mentioned that James Erskine must be considerably older than his wife, but at that time Sara had dismissed the fact as being of no concern to her. But now...

'How's Ben taking it?' James asked. 'I expect he's finding it a little strange too. Thank heavens he's so young. He'll recover so much easier.'

'I hope so.' Sara nodded. 'He and I will have to sort our future out fairly soon. We won't be going back to Brazil, of course. That goes without saying. But we have to find somewhere to live, and I have to find a job.'

'Of course.' A slight frown crossed his face for a moment. 'Well, if there's anything I—that is, Linda or I—can do, you must let us know.'

'Thank you.' Sara was genuinely sure that he meant it. 'It's very kind of you.'

'Not at all.' James patted her hand with gentle warmth. 'Ah—here comes my wife. I believe you've met her. And Alex. I'm sure he must be a tower of strength at this time.'

It wasn't a description that Sara would have used, but Linda's intervention forestalled any thoughts of that kind. 'Darling,' she said, touching her husband's hand, 'we should be going. We don't want to impose and—Sara!' Her start of surprise was almost convincing. 'I do apologise. I hadn't realised it was you James was speaking with. Let me offer my condolences. It was a terrible thing to happen. You must be quite distraught.'

'Yes.' Sara wished that she could respond with as much conviction. 'I—it was terrible. And so unexpected. Harry thought the men were his friends...'

Her voice was beginning to falter. In spite of herself the strain of the last few hours was getting to her, and the awareness of Alex, standing just behind Linda and listening to every word, was too much. In addition to which there was the unwarranted dislike she still felt for the other woman to cope with, made all the more contemptible because of her husband's kindness.

'Well, I'm sure James has told you that if there's anything either of us can do...' Linda added, her gracious tone grating on Sara's nerves. She tucked her arm into her husband's. 'Come along, darling. We've got the Websters coming at seven, remember?' She cast a challenging glance behind her. 'I'm sure we can leave Alex to take care of his sister-in-law.'

'Naturally.'

Alex's single word of acknowledgement set the seal on the Erskines' departure, but Sara was aware that James Erskine cast her another reassuring glance as he allowed his wife to usher him away. And it was some comfort to know that not everyone blamed her for what had happened to Harry. The Erskines were family friends, and could be relied upon to reflect the general mood.

Sara's concentration abruptly wavered. She wished she could make her departure too. This mannered observation of the required social protocol was beginning to tell on her, and now that Alex had resumed his position at her side she just wanted to be alone.

Watching James and Linda make their way to the door forced her to wonder what kind of relationship theirs was. She had heard of marriages where both partners lived their own lives, only staying together for personal reasons. Was Linda's interest in Alex only platonic these days, or was she still harbouring regrets of what could and should have been?

'You seemed to be getting along very well with James,' Alex observed, and the remark jarred on her already taut nerves.

'Is that a criticism?' she countered, her tiredness making her reckless. 'Don't judge everybody by your own standards, Alex. James Erskine seems an honourable man.'

Alex's mouth tightened for a moment. 'And I'm not?'

'I didn't say that.' Sara was quite proud of her look of indifference. 'I was merely being polite. I liked him. I can see why Linda married him.'

'Can you?' Alex was sardonic now. 'For the same reasons you married Harry, perhaps. Because—life—hadn't quite worked out as you planned.'

Sara's nails dug into her palms. 'You'd like to think so,' she hissed, and they both knew that they weren't talking about the Erskines now. 'Just keep away from me, Alex. I can do without your amateur psychology. Save it for Linda. I'm sure she's far more interested than me.'

Alex's fingers closed around her upper arm. 'Cool it, will you?' he said in a low, harsh voice. 'This isn't the place to have this discussion. I'm sure you don't want to embarrass the old man.'

'What old—? Oh, you mean your father.' Sara made an unsuccessful effort to get free, and then stood motionless in his grasp. 'Let me go. I have to go and check on Ben again. He'll be tired. It's past time for his nap.'

'He can wait.' But Alex released her anyway, realising, she was sure, that any possessive moves on his part could be badly misconstrued. 'Sara, we have to talk, you know. You can't keep putting it off.'

Sara swung away. 'I'm not putting anything off,' she retorted, aware that she was overreacting but unable to do anything about it. 'I don't need anything from you, Alex. I never did.'

The kitchen, when she reached it, was blessedly quiet and normal. The mingled smells of newly baked bread and pastry were deliciously familiar, bringing back a score of memories of when she was a child at home.

Unfortunately her childhood had been short-lived. Her parents had been killed in a car crash when she was barely ten, and as there had been no convenient relatives to look after her a series of foster homes had followed. At sixteen she had left that kind of protective custody for good and had found herself temporary accommodation in a hostel. With some luck, and a lot of hard work, she had eventually trained as a secretary, and by the time she'd met Harry she had attained the dizzy heights of personal assistant to a rather humble official in the social services.

Which was why Elizabeth Reed hadn't approved of
their association. A fairly ordinary girl from what she
regarded as a doubtful background was not what she
had had in mind for her son. Linda Erskine had been
only one of the contenders. Mrs Reed had paraded a
selection of would-be candidates before both Harry and
Alex. She'd wanted to ensure the purity of her grand-
children, thought Sara ruefully. Even Ben, enchanting
as he was, must give her some doubts.

But now was not the time to worry about that particular bugbear, or about any future bones of con-
tention that she might face about Ben's education. Both
of the Reeds' sons had gone to boarding-school as soon
as they'd been old enough, whereas Harry—and Sara
herself—had been adamant that Ben should continue to
live at home.

As she shut the kitchen door behind her she realised
that her son was not in the room. She had been hoping
to see Ben's cheerful little face, but instead all she saw
was Alison, Mrs Fraser's assistant, wiping down the table
where the bread-making had been taking place.

'Oh, hello, Mrs Reed,' Alison greeted her warmly. 'I
expect you're wondering where Ben's gone.'

'Well...' Sara arched a questioning eyebrow. 'I know
he can be quite a handful. Particularly when it's time
for his nap.'

'That's exactly what Mrs Fraser said,' declared Alison,
straightening from her task and flexing her back tiredly.
'So she's put him down for an hour, just to save you
the trouble. She's up there now, as it happens. Reading
him a story, I shouldn't wonder.'

'Oh—thanks.'

Sara was relieved. For a moment she had wondered
if the two women had let Ben go wandering off on his
own. But she should have known better, she reflected.
Although Alison was younger than she was, Mrs Fraser

had told her that she already had a couple of children of her own, and she was supplementing the rather modest income her husband made as a farm-worker by helping out at Perry Edmunds whenever she could.

'He's a nice little boy,' Alison added now, clearly willing to take a break. 'Rattles away nineteen to the dozen with us, he does. Been telling us all about where you used to live, and what him and his daddy used to do—'

She broke off abruptly as the realisation of what she had said brought a surge of hot colour to her cheeks. 'Oh, Mrs Reed!' she exclaimed. 'I didn't mean—that is, I didn't think.' She chewed at her lower lip anxiously. 'What must you think of me?'

'I think you and Ben must have got along famously,' said Sara, with a warm smile. 'And it's natural that Ben should talk about his father. I don't want him to feel it's a forbidden subject.'

'No, but—'

'I understand, Alison. I really do. And I hope you won't feel that you can't mention Harry's name to me either. What happened—well, it was—awful. But I have to go on living, and so does my son.'

Alison nodded. 'All the same, I wouldn't like you to think . . .'

'I don't think anything,' Sara reassured her gently. 'Just go on treating Ben like one of your own children. I'm sure you're making him feel really at home.'

Leaving the kitchen again—mainly to relieve Alison's embarrassment—Sara started up the back stairs. She had no desire to rejoin the gathering downstairs, and, although she knew that she would have to sooner or later, for the present she decided that a pretended visit to the bathroom would provide an excuse.

She met Mrs Fraser coming down, and after exchanging a few words about her son with the other woman she continued upstairs. The news that Ben had crashed out didn't surprise her. She herself was still feeling the effects of the jet lag, and his system was so much more delicate than hers.

She paused on the small landing that overlooked the gardens at the back of the house and gazed somewhat disbelievingly at the view. It had begun to rain a little now; the lawns and the paddock beyond were particularly English in appearance, and it seemed incredible how swiftly her life had changed in such a very short time.

Reaching the main landing, she made her way to the suite of rooms that the Reeds had allocated to her. They had been Harry's rooms, she knew, when he was alive, and although it was many years since he had lived at home their décor had changed little in the interim. His school sports pictures still adorned the walls of his study, which had been converted into a bedroom for Ben, and the toys he'd once played with had been saved for posterity, though Sara didn't think they'd interest his son.

The sound of the television was the first thing that Sara heard when she entered her apartments, and she went quickly to the door of Ben's room. Just as she'd thought, the old black and white set was on, though her son was lying motionless on his bed. She assumed that Mrs Fraser must have left it on for him—for company, perhaps—but as she went to turn off the rather violent cartoon that was playing the boy spoke, startling her.

'Can't I have it on?'

Sara swung round. 'I thought you were asleep. Mrs Fraser said...'

'I was—for a bit,' admitted the little boy, hauling himself into a sitting position. 'But I heard cars moving outside, and I went to see who was leaving, and then I just thought I'd see what was on.'

There was a certain diffidence in this statement, and Sara felt a sense of compassion for the child. He knew better than anyone that his father hadn't liked him to spend his time glued to the box, and generally he'd been outdoors, either in the swimming pool or in the garden, playing with the children of other members of the mission staff.

But he couldn't play outdoors here—not right now, at least. It was too cold for one thing, and for another he didn't know any of the children in the area. In addition to which there was no pool, no tropical gardens, no toys of his own to play with. Their personal belongings were coming by sea and were probably still in the middle of the Atlantic.

Deciding that the rules had to be changed here, along with everything else, Sara's lips tipped into a rueful smile and she left the television on. It was going to be hard enough for Ben to adjust without her stifling any independence he showed.

She nodded now, grimacing at the images on the screen but not making the mistake of switching channels and expecting him not to notice. Ben was fairly shrewd, and there was no way that she could alter the programme without his approval—not unless she used a heavy hand, which was something she hoped to avoid.

'Don't you like the Slime Monster, Mum?' he asked, wriggling round to look at her, and Sara pulled a wry face.

'Does anyone?' she asked. And then, sitting on the end of the bed, she went on, 'I want to talk to you. Do you think we could turn it off for a while? There's something I want to say.'

Ben grimaced. 'I s'pose so.'

'Good.' Sara leant across and did just that. 'It's difficult to think with that racket going on.'

Ben shrugged. 'It's just a cartoon, Mum.'

'I know.'

'But you don't think Dad would like it, hmm?'

Sara hesitated. 'I'm sure he wouldn't. And...' She paused. 'It's about Daddy that I want to talk to you—' She broke off again. 'This was his study, you know. When he was a boy. He used to do his homework here.'

'But Daddy said he went away to school.'

'Yes, he did.'

'Did he have homework in the holidays?'

'I'm not sure.' There were times when Sara wished that her son weren't quite so bright. 'In any event he kept his toys here. And those are his pictures on the walls.'

'Mmm.' Ben looked about him. 'They're very old, aren't they? Sort of yellow at the edges.'

'Not that old,' declared Sara painfully. 'Your father was still a young man when he—' She broke off once again and swallowed. 'Ben, can we talk about now? About why we're here?'

Ben frowned. 'This used to be where Daddy lived, isn't it? Before he went to live in Br-Bra—zil? When will we be going back to see him? Didn't he mind that we came such a long way?'

'No, he didn't mind,' said Sara, wondering how she could possibly tell the little boy that his father had flown back with them. How did she tell him about the shooting? Or convey the finality of Harry's death? She licked her lips. 'And...we won't be going back.' She chickened out at the sight of the dismay on his small face. 'Well...not for...not for a while anyway.'

'We're staying here?'

Ben was evidently trying to come to terms with what his mother was saying and Sara bit her lip.

'For a few days, maybe,' she conceded gently. 'Then— then you and I are going to find a home of our own.'

'Without Daddy?'

Sara sighed. 'Daddy's gone, Ben.' She paused again. 'Grandmama told you that.'

'Did she?' Sara didn't know whether to be relieved or sorry that Elizabeth Reed's harsh words had made so little impression on her son. 'Where's he gone? Why can't we go with him? He promised to get me a bicycle for my birthday.'

Sara almost smiled. It would have amused Harry too, she knew, and that made it harder to cope with—that his death should have been reduced to the loss of a bicycle. Yes, that was the real tragedy—that Ben had depended on him for the little things in his life as well as the big ones.

'Well,' she said, 'we'll have to see about that. And no, we couldn't go with him. Daddy's gone to heaven, with my mummy and daddy. They're probably watching us at this moment, and saying what a good boy Ben has been.'

'Are they?' Ben's face brightened up. 'Why didn't I see your mummy and daddy?'

'Because they went to heaven before you were born,' replied Sara with more confidence. 'Now, why don't you settle down for a nap? Then you can come and see Grandmama and Grandpapa before supper.'

'And Uncle Alex?'

Sara stiffened. 'Maybe.'

'He didn't get here until we went to that church thing,' declared Ben importantly. 'Grandmama said he's Daddy's brother.' He frowned. 'He hasn't gone to heaven too?'

'No.' Though Sara thought rather uncharitably that it would have been fairer if he had. Harry had never betrayed anyone. Yet he had been the one to die. She bit back the urge to tell her son not to depend on Alex— for anything—and forced a thin smile. 'So . . . we'll talk some more later. Let me take off your sweater. You don't need that on under the quilt.'

'Can I have the television on again? It might help me to go to sleep,' suggested Ben appealingly, and because it was the lesser of the two evils Sara agreed. She'd rather he was thinking of slimy monsters than his uncle Alex, though, come to think of it, she appended grimly, they had a lot in common.

She pulled his door to behind her and then spent a few minutes attending to her own appearance. Perhaps if she'd worn a brighter lipstick she wouldn't have looked so colourless, she mused doubtfully. But what did it matter anyway? She didn't care what anyone but Harry thought.

The room was cool, even though a check on the heavy old iron radiator elicited the information that it was working. But in a room of this size two or more radiators were needed, and she was almost glad to seek the comparative warmth of the hall outside.

Going down the main staircase this time, she was aware of the draught of cooler air from the open doors. The guest—*mourners*—were leaving, and the dampness from outside was spreading into the house.

'Oh, there you are, Sara!' exclaimed Elizabeth Reed, making her way towards her, her expression mirroring the disapproval that was evident in her voice. 'I think you might have stayed around a little longer. We all appreciate your position, but it would have been more polite.'

'I went to check on Ben,' said Sara stiffly, trying not to resent the older woman's attempts to put her in her place. Mrs Reed was suffering; that was obvious. Harry had been their older son, and it always hurt to lose one's child—of any age.

'Even so...'

The presence of remaining friends and neighbours prevented a prolonged protest, and Elizabeth's face resumed its gracious expression as she bid them goodbye. When remarks were addressed to Sara she offered her daughter-in-law regretful sympathy, and only she and Sara were aware of how insincere it was.

Alex was standing with his father, and for a brief moment Sara glimpsed the sorrow in his face. For all her own resentment towards him, she couldn't help but be aware of his feelings, and despite the animosity she felt towards him she couldn't deny a certain sympathy for his grief. Harry had been his brother, after all, and during the early years of their life they had spent a lot of time together.

Ironically enough, for all that he had been the elder, Harry used to say that it had been Alex who had defended him in times of schoolboy rivalry, which wasn't so surprising when you considered that Alex was probably two or three inches taller than his brother had been, and infinitely more muscular.

Feeling suddenly weary, Sara waited until the last guest had departed and then said carefully, 'If you don't mind, I think I'd like to have a rest before supper too.' She moistened her lips. 'I suppose it's partly the jet lag, but right now I feel really...exhausted.'

Robert Reed came to her support. 'Of course we don't mind, Sara,' he said, forestalling whatever comment his wife had been about to make. 'It's been a hard day for all of us. I'm sure we'd all appreciate a little time on our own.'

'Is Ben all right?'

Alex's unexpected question disconcerted her, and Sara turned to look at him with guarded eyes. 'Of course,' she said. 'Why shouldn't he be? I'm hoping most of this has gone over his head.'

'Is that why you let him attend the funeral service?' enquired Alex coolly, and this time there was no way that Sara was going to take the blame.

'That wasn't my idea. It was your mother's,' she replied stiffly, ignoring Elizabeth Reed's reproving glare. 'Now, if you'll excuse me, I'll go to my room. As your father says, I would appreciate some time to myself.'

CHAPTER THREE

WHEN Sara opened her eyes again it was daylight—and not the grey, rain-washed twilight of a winter's afternoon but, if she wasn't mistaken, the brightness of a crisp November morning. Although she could hardly believe it, it seemed that she—and possibly Ben too—had slept for almost sixteen hours, and a glance at her watch confirmed as fact what an unfamiliar sense of optimism was telling her.

And she did feel rested, wonderfully so. Despite the fact that she had slept in her clothes, with just the fluffy feather duvet pulled over her, she felt thoroughly revitalised. More than ready to face whatever was in front of her, she thought. And infinitely more equipped to take control of her life.

And her son's, she appended vigorously, thrusting back the duvet and swinging her legs over the side of the bed. Last night she hadn't even felt the hard springs of the mattress, which she'd blamed for the poor rest she'd had thus far.

But when she thrust open the door to her son's bedroom his bed was empty. There was the imprint of his head upon the pillow, and when she hurried to touch the mattress it still felt warm, but of Ben there was no sign, and her heart accelerated uneasily. Dear heaven, it was barely half past seven. Where on earth could he be?

Telling herself not to panic, she went back into the larger room and struggled to find the shoes she had discarded the previous afternoon. She could hardly go

35

looking for her son in her stockinged feet, even if her racing pulse was telling her to do exactly that.

She was running a hasty comb through her hair when someone tapped at the door. 'Come in,' she called at once, hardly daring to believe that it might be Ben playing a game. And it wasn't; it was Mrs Fraser, carrying a tray of morning tea and looking decidedly surprised to find Sara out of bed.

'Och, the little one said you were still asleep!' she exclaimed, and Sara saw the faintly puzzled glance she cast over her attire. She was probably wondering whether Sara intended to wear the black dress until it dropped off her, the younger woman thought ruefully. But her mention of Ben was reassuring, and Sara hurriedly put down the comb.

'You've seen Ben?'

'Well, yes.' Mrs Fraser put the tray down on the bedside table and turned to nod consideringly. 'He was up and about half an hour ago. He came down to the kitchen to tell me he'd had enough sleeping time and he was hungry.'

Sara relaxed. 'Thank heavens.' She glanced down at the creased black dress and grimaced. 'I was coming to look for him, actually. I was afraid he might have ventured outside on his own.'

'Ah.' Mrs Fraser's response was understanding. 'Well, you've no need to worry. The little one's in safe hands. His uncle Alex was up at the crack of dawn himself, and he's taken the youngster down to the stables.'

'Alex?'

Sara's reaction was only belatedly controlled, but she thought Mrs Fraser hadn't noticed anything amiss.

'Yes. The two of them settled for a bowl of my porridge and a mug of coffee, and then hied themselves off to see Dragonfly's filly.'

Sara swallowed. 'Dragonfly's a horse, right?'

'A mare,' agreed Mrs Fraser comfortably. 'The filly's sire is Dream Maker—young Alex's stallion. He was telling the lad about it and Ben fairly begged to see it.' She chuckled. 'He reminds me of his uncle, he does. Wants things yesterday, if not sooner.'

Sara endeavoured to speak calmly. 'Wasn't...wasn't Harry like that too? When he was younger?'

Mrs Fraser sensed that she had been a little insensitive, and offered Sara a rueful look. 'Bless you, no,' she said. 'Harry was always the patient one. The nicest-natured boy I ever met. That was your young man.'

Another thought struck Sara. 'Last night—that is...Ben didn't get up again either, did he?'

'No.' Mrs Fraser rested her hands on her hips. 'Both of you were sleeping as sound as tops when Alison looked in on you. That would have been about a quarter to eight last evening. When Mrs Reed was anxious to get supper over.'

'Oh, dear.' Sara could imagine that that was another black mark against her, but it was too late to worry about it now. She had more immediate worries to deal with— not least her son's apparent attachment to his uncle. Why couldn't he have attached himself to his grandfather— or even his grandmother, if he had to?

'Not to worry,' declared the Scots housekeeper staunchly. 'There's worse things than missing a meal, particularly when... Well, least said, soonest mended— that's what I always say. But you must be hungry yourself now. How'd you like a couple of nice poached eggs on toast, with some of Alison's jam to follow?'

'Well...'

'I could bring it up for you, of course,' went on the housekeeper. 'And maybe you'd prefer a pot of coffee as well. Something warming to start the day. You'll cope with everything so much better if you have some food inside you.'

Sara hesitated. Despite what she'd like to do, there was no way that she could go rushing after Ben and Alex without creating something of a fuss. Besides, where was the harm, for heaven's sake? Alex was the boy's uncle. Maybe he was beginning to regret that he hadn't married too.

And the idea of shedding her clothes and taking a hot shower while Mrs Fraser prepared her breakfast was appealing. Even the food sounded almost palatable. Good old British eggs that didn't swim in water on your plate.

'Why not?' she conceded at last, approaching the tea-tray with some affection. 'You're spoiling me, Mrs Fraser. I'm going to have to get used to managing on my own.'

Mrs Fraser hesitated herself now, then went to the door. But then, as if compelled to say something, she paused. 'Now, I don't imagine Mr and Mrs Reed will let that happen,' she declared, unaware of how disturbing her words were to Sara. 'That little boy's their grandson. They won't want to let him out of their sight.'

A cup of tea and a revitalising shower later, Sara was more prepared to view the Scotswoman's words without distress. Goodness, Mrs Fraser had no idea how the Reeds felt, or their daughter-in-law either. If Sara chose to move away there was nothing anyone could do about it.

In consequence she made a fairly creditable attempt at the poached eggs she found waiting for her, warm beneath a silver dome. Because she didn't want the food to get cold she merely pulled a Paisley-patterned wrapper about her before tackling her breakfast, and she was enjoying her second cup of coffee when Ben burst through the door.

'Mum! Mum!' For all that she had warned him a dozen times at home in Rio not to run about the villa, when he was excited he still forgot to control his feet.

He bounded into the room, an excited bundle of cold air and enthusiasm, coming to a halt abruptly when he saw that she was sitting on the bed. 'Mum, can I go out with Uncle Alex on a horse?'

Sara's brief sense of sanguinity dispersed. 'How many times—?' she began, choosing the least controversial response she knew of, and then caught her breath abruptly at the sight of the man who had paused by the open door.

'A pony, actually,' said Alex evenly, propping one broad shoulder against the frame. 'Good morning, Sara. You look...rested. Mrs Fraser said you were awake.'

Sara's lips tightened. 'But not prepared for visitors,' she said through teeth that threatened to split her tongue. 'Close the door, if you don't mind. I'm sure we can discuss this later. And Ben, your shoes are dirty. Get off the bed.'

Alex looked as if he might say something rather unpleasant, but courtesy—or merely iron control—won the day. With a faint smile he reached into the room and swung the door towards him, stepping out of its way as it thudded against the jamb.

'Oh, Mum!' Ben's reaction was much less restrained, his eyes sparkling instantly with unshed tears. 'Mum, I want to go now. Uncle Alex said I can if you'll let me.' He sniffed. 'Now you've gone and spoiled everything. I 'spect he's gone away.'

'He's gone downstairs, Ben, that's all,' said Sara, with rather less tolerance than she usually showed for her son's distress. 'For heaven's sake, you can't expect to burst in here and get your own way, all without even wishing me good morning. You shouldn't have left these rooms without my permission. I told you that when we first arrived.'

'You were asleep,' said Ben sulkily, scuffing what looked suspiciously like a smear of manure against the cinnamon-coloured pile of the carpet.

'Don't do that!' exclaimed Sara shortly. 'And have you had a wash this morning?' She frowned. 'I bet you haven't even cleaned your teeth, have you? What would your grandmother think?'

'I don't care,' mumbled Ben, pushing himself away from the bed and dragging his feet across the floor. 'Uncle Alex didn't care if I'd had a wash or not. And nor did Dragonfly or her foal.'

Sara sighed. 'All the same...'

Ben paused by the window. Drawing the curtain aside, he hunched one shoulder against the wall. Just like Alex, thought Sara helplessly. God, the sooner they left the better.

'Anyway,' she said, feeling obliged to try and rectify whatever damage Alex had done, 'I thought you and I might go shopping this morning. You haven't been to Newcastle. You never know, Father Christmas may have arrived.'

'Father Christmas?' Ben turned, trying to sound indifferent but not quite succeeding. 'Where?'

'At one of the stores in Newcastle,' declared Sara, hoping that she wasn't being premature. 'I know he used to turn up in London about this time. I don't see why it should be any different here.'

Ben frowned. 'But how can he be in London and Newcastle?' he exclaimed. 'You said London's a long way from here.'

'It is.' Sara finished her coffee, put the cup back on the tray and got to her feet. 'But Father Christmas is magic, isn't he? He can be everywhere, not just in one place.'

'Like God?'

Ben could be painfully logical when he chose, and Sara half wished she hadn't started this. 'No,' she said. 'Not like God. God lives in heaven. Father Christmas lives at the North Pole. With all the fairies and elves.'

Ben trudged back to the bed. 'Is Daddy with God?' he asked, and Sara realised that in explaining one problem she had created another. 'Uncle Alex says that Daddy won't be coming back. That he and Grandmama and Grandpapa are our family now.'

Sara expelled an uneven breath. 'Did he?' she said, wishing that Alex would just leave them alone. 'Well, of course they are. But not like Daddy and me and you. We—' she pointed a finger at the little boy's jersey and then at herself '—have to stick together. You'd like us to have a home of our own, wouldn't you? Just like we had before?'

Ben looked at her with solemn eyes. 'But it's not like it was before, is it?' he said, as if it were she who didn't understand. Then, with a sudden switch, he begged wheedlingly, 'Can't I go riding with Uncle Alex? I don't like shopping. I'd rather stay at home.'

The words This isn't your home! trembled on Sara's tongue, but she managed to restrain them. It was going to be hard enough dealing with Elizabeth Reed *with* Ben on her side. It would be impossible if she alienated him as well.

'We'll see,' she managed at last, as if there were all the time in the world to decide—and with that Ben had to be content. But he fussed about her as she was changing, evidently eager to resume his budding friendship with his uncle.

Using the tray as an excuse, Sara chose to use the back stairs to reach the kitchen, with Ben fretting at her heels. With a bit of luck Alex would have got tired of waiting and departed. She remembered Harry telling her that his brother was keen on horses, though these days he was seldom at home.

Which reminded her of something Alex had said the day before, and which until now had remained dormant. He'd said he'd bought *Ragdale*! What was she supposed to think of that?

As she had expected, there was no sign of Alex in the kitchen, and when Ben demanded to know where he'd gone Mrs Fraser couldn't tell him. 'He may have gone over to the Erskines',' she said thoughtfully. And to Sara she added, 'He sometimes goes for a swim in their pool. Mrs Erskine—she's always glad of the company. That husband of hers works every hour God sends.'

Ben's face dropped. 'But he was going to take me for a ride,' he protested loudly, tears again not far from being shed. He turned to his mother as if it was her fault— which, strictly speaking, Sara supposed it was—and sniffed dejectedly. 'Now what am I going to do? You should have let me go.'

Mrs Fraser arched an enquiring brow, but Sara was beginning to feel besieged and she had no intention of explaining herself to the housekeeper. 'Come along,' she said. 'You haven't said good morning to your grand-mother. Is she in the morning room, Mrs Fraser?'

'No, Mrs Reed. She's not up yet, I'm afraid. These days Mrs Elizabeth tends to take things more easily. She's almost sixty, you know, though she wouldn't like me to say so.'

Almost sixty! Of course; Sara supposed she must be. Yet when she had first come here Harry's mother had seemed so much younger than fifty-four. But time, and Harry's death, had to have taken their toll of his parents as much as anyone, and she decided that she must try to be more charitable when dealing with her mother-in-law.

Ben hunched his shoulders. 'I'd have liked to go swimming too,' he muttered, drawn again to his own grievances. 'Where do the Erskines live?' He looked up at his mother. 'Couldn't we go and find him? I bet he wouldn't mind. He said he wished he had had a boy like me.'

Sara's mouth dried at these words, but it was easier to address his earlier complaint. 'I don't think Mrs Erskine would be terribly pleased to see us, Ben,' she declared crisply. And, at Mrs Fraser's questioning look, she went on, 'She doesn't have any children of her own, does she?'

'Did Alex tell you that?' Mrs Fraser folded her arms, as she was inclined to do when she had some pearl of wisdom to impart. 'No, the Erskines don't have any family. But I hear it was a definite decision on their part.'

Sara's lips parted. The temptation to ask what the other woman meant by that remark was appealing, but she had no wish for her curiosity to be passed on. She could just imagine Elizabeth Reed's indignation if she learned that her daughter-in-law had been gossiping with the servants, and although Mrs Fraser was trustworthy her opinions weren't always discreet.

'Oh, well,' Sara said now, grasping Ben's hand firmly and heading towards the hall door. 'We'll just have to go shopping, as I suggested. Are there any buses to Newcastle, Mrs Fraser?'

'There are.' But Mrs Fraser looked doubtful about this. 'Perhaps you should see what Mrs Elizabeth says. I don't think she'd expect you to use the buses. If you're set on going shopping, someone should take you in the car.'

'I can drive, Mrs Fraser.' Sara was trying hard not to feel resentful. Was she really expected to clear all her movements with Harry's mother? She could feel her bid for independence slipping away. 'Perhaps I could borrow a car instead?'

Mrs Fraser was looking increasingly anxious, and, realising that she couldn't expect any satisfaction from this source, Sara made some remark about going to find Mr Reed and left the room. Surely Robert Reed didn't stay in bed until mid-morning? Harry had told her that even though he was semi-retired Robert played an active role in the administration of the estate.

She was crossing the hall and reminding herself that she must remember to wear a sweater over her shirt when the front door opened. Ben's accompanying tirade was immediately cut off as the object of his recriminations came casually into the house. Still wearing the black jeans and leather jacket that he had worn to her room earlier, Alex brought with him the sharp air of the morning and a not unpleasant scent of the outdoors.

'Uncle Alex, Uncle Alex!' Dragging his hand out of his mother's grasp, Ben darted to meet him, looking up at the man delightedly, as if he were some kind of god. It was obvious that the boy was missing his father, but did he have to treat Alex so affectionately? wondered Sara with a sense of gloom. It made her feel like the wicked stepmother in some silly Victorian melodrama.

'Now, then.' Alex greeted his nephew with an equal amount of affection, swinging the child up into his arms and grinning into his excited face. 'Does this mean we can go riding? Have you got your mother's permission at last?'

'No, he hasn't,' said Sara tersely, the sight of the boy and man together doing unpleasant things to her insides. 'I—Ben and I are going shopping. We need warmer clothes than those we've got at present.'

Ben's cry of outrage only narrowly missed being echoed by his uncle. 'Shopping?' he exclaimed. 'Can't you go shopping tomorrow? It's a beautiful morning. It's a shame to waste it going into town.'

Sara's lips tightened. 'Nevertheless—'

'Nevertheless—what?' Alex's expression had hardened somewhat. 'Is it really necessary to punish the child because you're angry with me? I've said we need to talk, and I mean it. So don't make me say something now we'll both regret.' He paused. 'I'll ask again; may I take Ben out for an hour or so this morning? I'm sure you can find other things to do.'

Sara's resentment was crippling, but there was no mistaking the threat in Alex's voice. She didn't know exactly what he meant—what he *knew*—but she couldn't risk him saying anything controversial in front of her son. 'I... Oh, very well.' She gave in ungraciously. 'But I shall hold you personally responsible for his safety; is that understood?'

'Of course.' Alex's dark eyes were vaguely sardonic.

'And... and how come you've got a pony for him to ride? I thought your father only bred hunters.'

'He does.' Alex set Ben on his feet and then regarded her steadily. 'We're boarding it while the bailiff's son and his family are away. Don't worry. I'll see Ben comes to no harm. He is the parents' only grandchild, after all.'

Sara turned away. She didn't need a reminder that, for all that she had longed desperately for another child, there had been no more pregnancies after Ben. Not that Harry had ever reproached her, she remembered. On the contrary, he had always assured her that he was content with the child they had. But then, Harry had always been there for her, in whatever way she needed him...

'He'll need to wear something warm.'

Alex's voice followed her as she moved across the polished floor, and she glanced round, beckoning Ben to come to her side. 'He doesn't have a hat,' she said, her voice clipped and flat. 'I thought that was essential before you got on a horse.'

'It's a pony, Mum!' exclaimed Ben, but Alex's reply overrode him.

'He can borrow Robin's. I'm pretty sure it will fit. Robin's only eight, you see. And rather small at that.'

'Come on, Mum!'

Ben's impatience was showing, and despite her reluctance she allowed him to tug her towards the stairs. 'You—you will look after him, won't you?' she demanded at last. She twisted her hands together. 'He's never been on a horse before. Harry—Harry was never very interested in—in animals.'

'I know.' Alex's eyes were guarded. 'He was my brother for twenty-eight years before he was your husband. I knew everything there was to know about him. Including his weaknesses...but I don't suppose you want to hear about them.'

CHAPTER FOUR

SARA sat before the mirror of the dressing table and tried to concentrate on applying some make-up. Already the slight tan she'd always worn was fading from her cheeks, the sun here lacking warmth, the chill of the old house accentuating her pallor.

She wasn't looking forward to going down to supper, but she couldn't avoid the evening meal a second time. Last night she'd had some excuse—she'd just buried her husband, for heaven's sake. But this evening she was supposed to be coming to terms with the situation, exercising that stiff upper lip.

A sudden surge of grief overtaking her, Sara pressed her lips together. God, if only there were someone she could share her feelings with. Mrs Fraser had come the nearest to showing any understanding, but was she just being polite to her employers' daughter-in-law?

She had thought that Ben might compensate in some way for Harry's absence, but he seemed to have adapted quickly to his changing circumstances. Today, for instance, she'd hardly seen him, what with him going out with Alex this morning, and then accompanying his grandmother for a walk with the dogs this afternoon. Oh, Elizabeth Reed had invited Sara to join them, but she'd found herself making some excuse. The truth was that she wasn't ready yet to let go of the past.

At least she hadn't had to spend the *whole* afternoon listening to what a paragon of all the virtues Ben's uncle Alex was. She had been forced to take an interest when Ben had explained his first lessons in the paddock, but when he'd gone on to describe what a 'super' rider his uncle was and what a 'terrific' horse he had Sara had switched off. She only hoped that she could keep her patience until they could comfortably leave.

The sound of splashing from the bathroom reminded her that her son was presently waiting for her to take him out of the bath. Ben had already had his supper, and had been unexpectedly quiescent about having an early night. She ought to be grateful that he was adapting to going to bed at a normal time. In Brazil he'd often slept the afternoon away, and then been under their feet half the evening.

Leaving her lipstick to be applied later, Sara rose to her feet, smoothing the black silk slip down over her narrow hips. She wasn't wearing a bra, and the cool air had hardened her nipples, turning them into provocative peaks that pushed against the fabric.

It was the only sign that that part of her anatomy wasn't as numb as the rest of her, she thought. Since Harry's death she'd felt frozen—except when Alex tied knots in her nerves.

'Time to come out,' she said now, forcing a smile as she entered the adjoining bathroom. Like the rest of the apartments, it had suffered from ageing, and the claw feet of the bath were a danger to unwary toes.

'Oh, must I?' Like all small boys, Ben enjoyed playing in the water, and Mrs Fraser had unearthed an old boat and a pair of rubber ducks that Harry used to enjoy.

'Bless you, he had fun with those ducks for more years than he'd like to remember, I dare say,' the housekeeper had told the little boy ruefully. 'I'd stow them away in the cupboard, but he'd haul them out again.'

'I'm afraid you must,' declared Sara in answer to her son's plea, feeling her skin burst into goose-bumps as the moist steam touched her flesh. She had him stand up, and then wrapped him in a towel and carried him into the bedroom. Ironically this room was warmer. It didn't have so many draughts from the windows.

Someone knocked at the door as she was buttoning Ben into his pyjamas, and, assuming it was Mrs Fraser, she barely hesitated before calling, 'Come in.'

But it wasn't Mrs Fraser, it was Alex, and Ben couldn't wait to scramble down from her knee. 'Did you come to say goodnight?' he exclaimed as Sara remained with her back to the door and wrapped her arms about herself in irritation. 'You can put me to bed, if you like. That's what Daddy used to do.'

'Ben!' Sara spoke through her teeth, and then, because it wasn't truly Ben's fault, cast a furious look over her shoulder. 'Do you mind going away? Or am I to have no privacy? The sooner we find our own place the better. I didn't know I was going to have to lock my door to keep people out.'

Alex's jaw hardened, but he didn't immediately beat a retreat. 'I came to tell you supper is ready,' he said flatly. 'Or were you planning on hiding up here again? I'm sorry; I assumed you'd be ready. It is half past seven.'

'Is it?' Sara's response was less acerbic now, and she glanced somewhat disbelievingly at her watch. She must have spent longer than she'd imagined studying her reflection, and now Harry's mother would think that she had planned her tardiness deliberately.

'Perhaps if I put Ben to bed while you put some clothes on?' suggested Alex coolly, but Sara knew that she couldn't allow that. Apart from how embarrassed she would feel at having Alex in the room while she got dressed, she could imagine her feelings if he teased the boy, started him laughing, just as if they were a family— She swallowed. Oh, no, that couldn't happen. It wouldn't do at all.

'If you'd just go, I'll be down directly,' she declared, making sure that she kept her back to him as she spoke.

What could he see, after all? Just her bare shoulders, and the narrow straps over them. Not the sensual thrust of her nipples that might give him entirely the wrong impression.

'All right.' Pulling a rueful face at Ben, Alex didn't argue, but when the door had closed behind him Sara had to face her son again.

'Why don't you like Uncle Alex?' he protested tearfully, but he was fortunately too tired to put up much of an effort. 'He's nice. I like him. He makes me think of Daddy. He makes me laugh.'

'Well, that's good,' said Sara, refusing in her turn to be too negative. 'But come along now. Grandmama's waiting. And we both know how impatient she can be.' Elizabeth Reed had chided her grandson for spending too long getting his boots on before their walk. She'd made the excuse that the dogs were getting anxious, but Sara suspected that she'd never had much patience where children were concerned.

Ben snuggled down beneath the covers without any further argument, and after bestowing a goodnight kiss Sara carefully closed the door. She had no reason now to dawdle, even if the alternative was hardly to her liking, and she had no wish to make an entrance, though she was afraid that she wasn't going to have much choice.

As far as choosing something to wear was concerned, that didn't take a lot of effort. The few suitable clothes she'd brought with her were mostly too thin or too casual. But she hadn't planned on much entertaining when she'd packed for Harry's funeral, and she'd also quite forgotten how cold this house could be.

Her choice—which wasn't really a choice after all—lay between the black dress that she had worn the day before and a dark green velvet tunic, whose hem seemed much too short. She really would have to try and get to the shops the following day, she thought impatiently.

She could imagine what Elizabeth would say when she saw an immoderate amount of thigh.

But the black dress was unwearable until it had been cleaned and pressed, and at least the velvet had long sleeves. She'd have worn it for the funeral if she hadn't been afraid of accusations of impropriety, and at least there were no visitors to comment on her appearance.

Nevertheless, as she descended the stairs she had the ridiculous urge to pull futilely at her hem. It didn't matter that she had added black opaque stockings that looked almost as thick as leggings. She still felt like a schoolgirl seeking the headmistress's approval.

Alison was just coming out of the library as Sara reached the hall, and her eyes lit up appreciatively. 'What a lovely dress,' she said, clearly considering herself out of Mrs Reed's hearing. 'They're waiting for you in there.' She twitched a shoulder towards the library door. 'Mr and Mrs Bowden are here. You'll have met the minister yesterday, I dare say.'

Sara uttered a decidedly unChristian oath under her breath at the news that it would not be just the family for supper. Was Elizabeth Reed totally without feeling? Didn't she realise that Sara needed some time to get over her grief?

Whether he had heard Alison speaking to her or had simply been watching out for her Sara wasn't sure, but Alex appeared at that moment. His tall frame blocked the crack in the door he had opened, and although it was the last thing that should have been on her mind she couldn't prevent the conclusion that dark colours suited him best. This evening he had shed the leather jacket and jeans for a charcoal-grey lounge suit, the collarless shirt beneath an indication that his mother hadn't chosen his clothes.

'Come and have a drink,' he said, easing her passage into the library. 'White wine, is it, or something else? Perhaps your tastes have changed.'

You wish, thought Sara uncharitably, but she accepted the wine without demur. There was little point in her choosing something stronger. She already felt a little light-headed as it was.

'You look nice this evening, my dear!' exclaimed Robert as his son went to get her drink. 'You remember Mr Bowden, don't you? And Helen, did you ever meet Harry's wife?'

'I don't believe so.' Helen Bowden smiled and offered a limp hand. In her middle forties, Sara guessed, she was one of those women who looked somewhere else when they were speaking to you—a result of too many social gatherings where boredom was high on the menu.

'I was just thanking...Charles—' Elizabeth Reed offered a coy smile to the vicar '—for the very tasteful way he conducted the service yesterday,' she said. 'I'm sure we're all agreed it was a sad occasion, but his words were a great comfort. Particularly at the graveside. Didn't you think so, Sara, my dear?'

'Oh—yes.' In truth, Sara could hardly remember anything of the funeral service at all. From the moment the coffin had been carried into the village church her emotions had been in chaos. There had been something so unreal about it. She'd found it hard to accept that Harry's body was in that anonymous box.

'I particularly liked the reading from Corinthians,' went on her mother-in-law imperviously. '"For now we see through a glass, darkly; but then face to face..."'

'Beautiful,' agreed Mr Bowden, nodding. 'And spoken with such feeling, Elizabeth. You put my poor efforts to shame, I'm sure.'

'Nonsense!' exclaimed Mrs Reed modestly. 'The Bishop himself couldn't have conducted the service any better. We're very lucky here at St Matthew's. That's why you have such an enthusiastic congregation every Sunday.'

'So kind, dear lady, so kind,' murmured the clergyman, but Alex, putting a glass of wine into Sara's hand, pulled a wry face.

'It couldn't be because the good Reverend flatters all the women outrageously,' he remarked in an undertone. 'The man's a veritable leech. He'd do anything to supplement his stipend.'

Sara didn't want to find anything Alex said amusing, but she couldn't deny the treacherous smile that tugged at her lips. 'I'm sure you're exaggerating,' she hissed, glancing somewhat apprehensively in the clergyman's direction. And then, meeting Robert Reed's knowing gaze, she coloured. 'In any case, I can't comment. I've only been to St Matthew's once.'

'Take my word for it,' murmured Alex, his eyes continuing their watching vigil of the rest of the group. He paused. 'Did Ben settle down without any trouble? He looked very tired to me.'

Sara had even less desire to get into a conversation with him about Ben, but although she cast a hopeful look in Robert's direction he had been cornered by Helen Bowden and was unlikely to help. 'He's asleep,' she said at last, when an answer became unavoidable. 'Tell me, is there a car I can borrow tomorrow?'

Alex's brows descended. 'A car?'

'Yes. You know, a four-wheeled vehicle with an engine and a steering wheel!' exclaimed Sara rather testily. 'I want to go to Newcastle. Is there anything wrong with that?'

'The shopping,' surmised Alex drily. 'Of course. I'd forgotten you'd planned to go today. But I think it did Ben good to get out and see a little of the countryside.

This is his heritage, after all, and he needs to feel at home.'

Sara endeavoured to speak calmly. 'I agree,' she said. 'It was his father's heritage, and I dare say you consider it's yours, but you have to remember that Ben's half Maxwell and I was born in London. He's just as much at home in the streets and squares of Fulham.'

Alex's expression tightened. 'As the kid hasn't had a really settled home since he was born, I hardly think he'll have made any distinction,' he snapped. 'All I'm saying is this place has roots; it has permanency. You're not going to tell me you found any roots in those foster homes you cherish!'

Sara caught her breath. 'How dare you?'

'How dare *you*?' retorted Alex with equal feeling. 'Forget it, Sara. He's staying here. Don't make me say too much.'

The appearance of Alison to say that the meal was ready was hardly a relief. Sara was shaking so much that she could hardly set her glass down without clattering it against the tray. As it was, Robert saw her difficulty and took the wineglass from her. 'Come along,' he said. 'Take my arm. I believe it's roast beef this evening. My favourite.'

Sara was grateful for his understanding, particularly as it left Helen Bowden to be escorted by Alex. Elizabeth Reed and the vicar were a natural pairing, and Sara couldn't help wondering if in that respect Alex was right.

Not that she wanted to admit that Alex might be right about anything, but at least it relieved her of the necessity of thinking about anything else. But after they were seated at the table, with Alex, happily, some distance diagonally from her, she found that his father wanted to talk about his grandson in a similarly proprietorial tone.

'Alex tells me he's a natural little horseman,' he remarked as Alison was serving the watercress mousse. 'We'll have to see about getting him a pony of his own. Tell me, Sara, did you ever learn to ride?'

At the social services' expense? Sara squashed the unworthy retort and shook her head. Robert was only being polite. He must know that her childhood had been vastly different from Harry's.

'Then you must learn,' her father-in-law insisted now. There's nothing like seeing the hills and valleys from the back of a horse. First thing in the morning, with the hounds fanning out from your heels. Let me tell you, my dear, it's a must.'

Sara caught her lower lip between her teeth. 'You mean hunting, don't you?'

Robert Reed frowned. 'Occasionally.'

'Then...' she hesitated '...I have to tell you, I don't agree with hunting for animals. I know all the arguments, but I wouldn't want to do it.'

Robert smiled. 'No one's asking you to, my dear. Don't you know Alex holds a similar view? And he was blooded when he was seven. His grandfather's suggestion, not mine, I might add.'

Sara breathed a little more easily. 'Anyway,' she said, 'I probably won't have time to take up your offer. As—as soon as—as soon as a decent interval has elapsed I'm hoping to move back to London. I'm sure I'll find it easier to get a job there, and Ben's old enough to go to kindergarten.'

'Did I hear you say kindergarten, Mrs Reed?' Helen Bowden had evidently tired of trying to draw Alex into conversation and was now leaning across the table towards her. 'Because I happen to know there's an excellent pre-school playgroup in Corbridge, and they're looking for new starters just now.'

'Oh, I—'

'Sara hasn't decided yet what she's going to do,' put in Robert swiftly, and Sara guessed that he'd spoken as much for his advantage as for hers. 'It may be easier to employ a nanny for Ben. Who knows? But thank you for your input, Helen. I'm sure we'll keep it in mind.'

Helen gave a vague smile and turned to the cream mousse on her plate. And, because she didn't want another argument, Sara did the same, though the food was like sawdust on her tongue.

By the time the roast beef was served the conversation had turned to the unstable situation in eastern Europe and Alex was being forced to share his personal experiences in Bosnia with the rest of the group. Against her will Sara found his caustic good sense appealing, his narrative spare and concise, but not lacking compassion. She remembered that it was what had caught her attention more than five years ago. She'd been flattered by his apparent interest in her, and had never stopped to ask herself why...

Mrs Fraser had completed the meal with a chocolate gateau—a dessert that brought many protestations of over-indulgence from Mrs Bowden. But Sara noticed that the lady managed two servings of the delicious concoction, her lips smeared unattractively with cream.

For herself she refused any of the dessert, having found even the roast beef and Yorkshire pudding beyond her. She reassured Robert that she was used to eating only vegetables and salads, but the truth was that her nerves had closed her throat.

With the meal over, they all adjourned from the rather gloomy confines of the dining room to the rather more cheerful aspect of the drawing room. Whoever had built Perry Edmunds all those years ago had evidently had a penchant for heavy panelling, and in consequence there was a predominance of gloom.

The drawing room was marginally brighter. There was no panelling here, but heavily embossed wallpaper in a rather daunting shade of burgundy that matched the heavy sofas and padded chairs. An open fire in the hearth gave an added warmth to the proceedings, and Sara edged as close to it as she dared while keeping an eye on Alex.

Alison brought in the tray of coffee and set it on the low table beside her mistress. 'If you want any more, Mrs Fraser says just to ring,' she announced, and then grinned at Sara encouragingly as she was leaving.

'That woman is too familiar!' exclaimed Elizabeth Reed as the door closed behind her. Ignoring her husband's resigned stare, she fussed with the coffee-pot, and gave Helen Bowden an enquiring glance. 'Don't you agree?' she asked, directing her attention to the cups. 'I'd prefer a younger maid if I could find one. Married women are too indifferent about their jobs.'

'I know what you mean—' began Helen, but Sara couldn't allow her mother-in-law's comments to go unchallenged.

'Well, I think Alison's charming,' she said. 'And she's very good with Ben. When there are children in the house, an older woman is more understanding. The girls we had in Rio were more interested in their appearance than in their work.'

Elizabeth fixed her with a haughty gaze. 'Well, I wouldn't know what things were like in Rio, of course,' she said, reminding Sara that she had never been invited to find out. Sara doubted whether she'd believe that that had been Harry's decision, not hers, but perhaps she should have insisted instead of giving in. 'In any event, your knowledge of the woman is hardly relevant. You've only known her a few days.'

'That may be true, but—'

'When you get to know my mother better you'll realise that it's genetically impossible for her to approve of the help,' remarked Alex coolly before an argument could ensue. 'We all know Alison does her job efficiently and intelligently. But if she knew that she might ask for a rise, and that wouldn't do at all.'

There was a general ripple of laughter, and even Elizabeth Reed thawed enough to smile at her son. 'What would you know?' she exclaimed. Then with rather more feeling she went on, 'You're never here. I always said that when Harry married Sara I lost both my sons at once.'

Robert Reed chimed in now. 'You didn't lose a son when Harry married Sara,' he protested, once more struggling to preserve an air of harmony. 'You gained a daughter, and now a grandson. You can't deny that Ben is a Reed through and through.'

Sara bent her head and studied the hearthrug. This was even harder than she'd thought it would be. What with Elizabeth chipping away at her confidence, and Alex like a predator, just waiting for her to make a mistake, she felt surrounded by enemies. Only Harry's father seemed to have any notion of how she was feeling, and even he had his own agenda where Ben was concerned.

Thankfully, Charles Bowden chose that moment to intercede with some comment of his own, and Sara guessed that he was feeling neglected. She'd already gathered that the Reverend enjoyed being the centre of attraction, and he was finding all this talk about families and servants very boring.

Helen Bowden took it upon herself to pass the cups of coffee around, and Sara drank hers with rather more speed than enjoyment. Then, returning the empty cup to the tray, she forced a polite smile.

'If you don't mind,' she said, remaining on her feet and pretending to stifle a yawn behind her hand, 'I am rather tired. Would you all excuse me?'

Elizabeth looked annoyed as the three men in the group were obliged to stand also. 'It's very early!' she exclaimed as the grandfather clock in the hall outside obligingly struck the half-hour. 'It is only half past nine, Sara. And you had an early night last night.'

'I'm sorry—'

'I'll escort Sara to her room, Mother,' put in Alex smoothly. 'I want to have a word about Ben's riding lessons anyway. I'm sure you won't miss us. You only need four for bridge.'

'Oh, really, I—'

Sara's attempted protest was swallowed by a chorus of approval from the other guests. 'You must let us try to recoup our losses, Elizabeth!' exclaimed Charles Bowden jovially. Then to Sara he went on, 'We only play for the thrill of it, of course.'

Sara looked at Alex. He had been seated across the hearth from her, but now he came with casual assurance to her side. He always moved like the sinuous predator she'd likened him to in her thoughts, she thought. But the mocking challenge in his eyes made her feel sick.

'You don't mind?' he asked, but she knew it was just a formality. He knew that there was no way she could attempt to oppose him here. Until she had a home of her own he'd always be able to play this cat-and-mouse game with her. Even his father would do nothing to oppose his son,

But then Robert didn't know, didn't even suspect that Alex might have any ulterior motives, Sara reminded herself grimly. So far as Harry's father was concerned, she and Alex barely knew one another. They were related by marriage, but that was all. Their association was impersonal, their contact brief.

'Do I have any choice?' she responded now, managing to inject her words with enough warmth not to alert his parents to how she really felt. 'But I doubt you'll get much sense out of me. I'm afraid I'm almost asleep on my feet.'

'We'll see,' said Alex pleasantly, and much to her annoyance he took her arm to lead her to the door. Even through the soft fabric she could feel the strength in his fingers. He was demonstrating his power, and she despised him for it.

CHAPTER FIVE

SARA awoke with a headache.

When she opened her eyes the morning light filtering through the curtains only added to the pounding in her head. It was after eight o'clock and it wasn't a particularly bright morning. But it was the presence of the day that filled her with apprehension.

And which had probably caused her headache, she acknowledged dully, levering herself up on her elbows. The action intensified the hammering in her skull, and she speedily sank down again. But not before the memory of the previous night assailed her, and caused a groan to issue from her lips.

Alex.

She drew a careful breath, and felt the hammering subside a little, although she still felt unpleasantly sick. Although she'd rarely had them before, she recognised the symptoms of a migraine. Oh, God, how could she go shopping in this state?

She groaned again, wondering if she had the strength to crawl out of bed and get some aspirin. Not that anything would really cure it, but it might help to ease the pain. The fact that she'd drunk several glasses of wine the night before with scarcely anything in her stomach was probably a factor in her nausea. She had never been a drinker, and the wine had been rather strong.

As she lay there feeling sorry for herself she wondered if Ben had obeyed her instructions. If he had, he would still be in his room, and, pushing the covers aside, she dragged herself to her feet. The pain was quite excruciating for a moment and she stood there, swaying. But as it gradually subsided again she padded across to his door.

Ben was just waking up. Evidently the jet lag was still affecting his sleeping habits—he had usually been up at seven o'clock at home in Rio—but at least he looked rested and deliciously tousled, and Sara thought how lucky she was to have such an adorable child.

'Are you all right, Mum?' he asked as she hovered in the doorway, and she explained about her headache with some regret. 'Hey, does this mean we don't have to go shopping?' Ben crowed. Then, with rueful diffidence, he added, 'Uncle Alex might take me out again, if it isn't raining.'

Frankly Sara felt as if she hadn't the strength to care what Alex did. After their confrontation last night she was in no doubt that as long as she stayed in Edmundsfield he had the upper hand. Which was another reason why she resented this headache. If the Reeds thought her health was suspect they'd never let her take Ben away.

'We'll see,' she said, and then winced as those words reminded her of Alex's implied threat of the night before. Though 'implied' was hardly the description to use. There'd been an overtly hostile conviction in his voice.

Of course, she'd been aware of the threat he represented long before she'd left Rio. Which was another reason—though not an excuse—why she had never tried to persuade Harry to invite his family to their home. Out of sight, out of mind, had been her maxim, though she had to admit that it hadn't been so easy in the beginning.

Still, Alex was not to know that, even if he did act as if he had some intrinsic knowledge that he didn't choose to convey. And if he did suspect the truth he could never say it, she'd argued with herself. His parents would never condone his actions, whatever excuses he gave.

Nevertheless, that didn't prevent him from treating her like an idiot. Whatever his parents thought about his behaviour—and there was no reason why they shouldn't accept it at face value—Sara knew what he was really thinking. If he couldn't get to her, he could get to her son. And Ben was the innocent pawn in this game.

Not that he had given her any reason to complain as they'd mounted the stairs together. And to give some credence to his ploy of wanting to talk to her about Ben's riding lessons she'd had to accept his company. But when they'd reached her apartments she'd had more sense than to invite him into them, determining to say goodnight without delay.

But Alex had had other plans.

'We need to talk,' he'd said flatly, not accepting her denial. And when she'd protested that they'd wake Ben he'd suggested that they go to his suite of rooms.

Sara had gasped. 'You have to be joking!' she'd exclaimed. 'I—I—I don't want to go to your rooms. We have nothing to say to one another. Besides,' she'd added, as this hadn't appeared to be making any impression, 'I thought you didn't live here. I thought you were over at Ragdale now.' For the first time the thought of the nearby house hadn't filled her with quite so much apprehension.

'I still stay here from time to time,' retorted Alex evenly, his hand about her upper arm offering little compassion. 'For God's sake, Sara, I'm not suggesting anything outrageous. Despite what you think of me, I have some respect for my brother's memory.'

'But not for his wife!' countered Sara tremulously, and Alex swore.

'You weren't his wife when I—when *we* knew one another. Now stop behaving like a silly little girl and come with me.'

Sara's mouth compressed. 'No.'

'Yes.' He was inflexible. 'I have to go to London in a couple of days, and I may not be back for over a week. I do not intend to allow this—this vendetta you're conducting to continue. Now for God's sake grow up and act like an adult.'

After that there was little Sara could say, short of proving herself the juvenile he'd implied. Besides, she told herself, she could do this. She was Harry's widow, not the wide-eyed innocent he'd first encountered.

Alex's sitting room was considerably warmer than the corridor had been, and whether he had had a hand in the decorations or not it was considerably more cheerful as well. The wallpaper here was much lighter—a creamy figured silk—and there was an attractive assortment of pictures to break up the daunting height of the walls. There was a beige and green striped sofa, two armchairs in green moiré, and a writing desk of generous proportions.

Even the rather grim expanse of beige carpeting had been hidden by a huge patterned rug. 'From Kashmir,' said Alex offhandedly, noticing her interest. Then he asked, 'Do you want a drink? I can't offer you wine, but I think I've got some brandy.'

'No, thank you.'

Sara was already feeling the effects of the wine she had drunk at supper. She didn't normally like red wine, but it had been served with the roast beef, and she'd needed something to lubricate her tight throat in order to try to eat. Not that she'd had much success. She'd kept emptying her glass but little else.

'Sit down.'

Alex indicated the sofa, and although Sara would have preferred to remain standing she subsided into a chair—but not one of the squashy moiré armchairs that were set too close together. She chose an upright carver, set squarely against the wall.

Meanwhile Alex helped himself to a brandy. Or at least he measured about an inch of the spirit into a glass he took from a drawer in his desk. Then, with a fairly sardonic glance at her choice of seating, he went to stand before the screened fireplace, which was an anachronism now in the centrally heated room.

She was aware that his dark eyes were appraising her as she sat there, looking anywhere but at him. He was probably speculating as to whether she was afraid of him. Well, she wasn't, she told herself grimly. She just couldn't relax when he was around.

'First of all, I want you to know that I was gutted when I heard about Harry's death,' he began at last, and she squeezed her hands together in her lap. 'I haven't had a proper chance to say how much I'm going to miss him. We hadn't seen one another much in recent years, but I loved him just the same.'

Sara had to look at him then. 'You hypocrite!' she said. 'You bloody hypocrite! You didn't love Harry. You only love yourself.'

'That's not true,' he intoned bleakly, not responding to her accusation in any way she had expected. 'You never knew my brother if you don't now believe we were close. Until you came along there'd never been a rift between us. You made that rift, not Harry, and not I.'

Sara started to get to her feet. 'I don't have to sit here and listen to this—'

'Yes, you do.' Alex's tone made her subside again. 'For God's sake, get things into perspective. What happened was...inevitable. There's no point in decrying it now.'

'That's your excuse, is it?'

'Dammit, it's not an excuse.' Alex's jaw clamped alarmingly. 'We were young—younger than we are now, that's for sure—and we were attracted to one another. It's not a thing I'm proud of, but it wasn't a hanging offence.'

'I doubt if Harry would have agreed with you.'

'Leave Harry out of this!'

'Why?' Sara's lips twisted. 'Is that the way you've dealt with it? By pretending it didn't matter because your brother never knew?'

'For God's sake, Sara, it wasn't like that!'

'Wasn't it?' Sara was beginning to believe that she could cope with this, as long as she kept her head. 'I think you behaved despicably. So don't talk to me about *love*!'

Alex shook his head. 'How you do delude yourself, Sara. Are you really trying to tell me you didn't want what happened as much as me?'

'Yes.' Sara was adamant. 'You took advantage of me; you took advantage of your brother. You *made* me do...do what I did. I'll never forgive you for it.'

Alex closed his eyes for a moment, and briefly she thought she'd won. But when they opened again they were dark with accusation, and she shrank from the fury in his face. 'You're crazy,' he said, his voice now harsh with loathing. 'If you hadn't been so damned provocative I'd never have touched you—may God forgive me!'

'God may forgive you but I won't,' declared Sara unsteadily, realising as she said the words how immature they sounded. He was right, she thought. She was behaving childishly. For Harry's sake she had to deal with these people, and bringing up old scores was hardly the most sensible thing to do.

'All right,' said Alex wearily, before she'd had a chance to redeem herself. 'It's obvious you've been avoiding the truth for so long that you're incapable of facing what really happened. It wasn't planned—on my part, at least. But don't pretend you weren't just as guilty as me.'

'All right.' Sara took a trembling breath, realising as she did so that she had confounded him at last. And then, because she wanted this to be over with, she tilted her head towards him. 'If that's all you wanted me to say, I'd like to go now.'

'It wasn't all.' Alex swore. 'Dammit, Sara—'

'Then can't it wait until tomorrow?' Sara managed not to show how anxious she still felt. 'I really am...exhausted...'

Alex swallowed a mouthful of his brandy and regarded her with darkened eyes. 'You're not making this any easier, Sara.' He shook his head. 'Harry's death...we were none of us prepared.'

'Can anyone be prepared for tragedy?' asked Sara bitterly. Her lips twisted. 'You were saying at dinner that you'd seen more than most.'

'Stop trying to score points, can't you?' Alex emptied his glass and went to pour himself another. He sighed. 'I actually brought you here to talk about Ben, not us. You'd agree he's the most important person now?'

'Of course.' On that at least he wouldn't get an argument. 'But Ben's OK. I'll see he doesn't suffer because of what's happened.'

Alex sighed. 'That wasn't quite what I meant.'

'No?' Sara avoided his chilling gaze. 'Well, if you're going to suggest buying him a pony, or some other expensive toy designed to get him to persuade me to stay here, forget it. As I said before supper—notwithstanding your threats—I don't intend to make my home in Northumberland.'

Alex's eyes narrowed. 'No?'

'No.' Sara was shaking a little now, and she made a play of pleating the folds of her skirt to give herself something to do. She had crossed her legs, but now she uncrossed them again, realising what an expanse of thigh she was displaying. Pressing both feet to the floor, she coaxed the velvet to her knees. 'I intend to get a job in London.'

'And leave Ben here?'

That suggestion was so outrageous that she was forced to lift her head. 'Of course not,' she said. 'Ben lives with me.' She swallowed. 'I can only assume you're joking. Well, let me tell you, it was in very bad—'

'I wasn't joking.' Alex's voice was flat. 'I think it's an eminently suitable arrangement. He's lived with you for the past four years. I think it's time he lived with his father.'

Sara's jaw dropped. 'I beg your—?' She gathered her scattered senses. 'Ben's father's dead.'

'Is he?' There was a depressing note of conviction in his words. 'We both know Harry wasn't Ben's father, so why don't we stop pretending? It's the cross I've carried with me for years.'

Now, standing in the doorway, the memory of that conversation made Sara groan again, and Ben sprang anxiously out of bed. 'What is it, Mum?' he asked fearfully. 'Have you got a pain or something? Shall I go and ask Mrs Fraser for some pills?'

Sara shook her head, wincing as she did so. 'No,' she said, trying to infuse some reassurance into her voice. 'It's just a headache. And I've got pills, darling. They're in my bag in there.' She lifted a shoulder towards her bedroom and Ben obediently scooted round her, enjoying the unfamiliar feeling of being in charge.

As Ben rummaged in her bag for the aspirin, and then went to get a glass of water from the bathroom for her to take them with, Sara crawled back into bed. Even without the bruising headache she'd have had some misgivings about leaving the bedroom. Oh, God, why had she come back here? She ought to have stayed away.

And she could have, she reflected bitterly. Without those desperate phone calls from Harry's mother she'd never have thought of bringing her husband's body back to England. It wasn't usually done. When expatriates died in tropical climates they were invariably buried with all speed. But Elizabeth Reed had insisted on contacting the authorities, and because of the circumstances special arrangements had been made.

Which was how she came to be here, trapped with the only man who could destroy her, and crippled by a migraine besides. How she'd got herself back to her own room the night before was still a mystery to her. But at least Alex had had the good sense not to try and stop her.

Perhaps he'd thought that she was going to throw up, she reflected weakly, and he hadn't wanted to have to explain that situation to his parents. Instead, after he'd delivered his bombshell, he'd let her escape without demanding a response. He'd probably assumed that she needed time to accept his terms.

Never, she thought now, her lips trembling as she swallowed two of the aspirin tablets that Ben had given her. She'd never accepted that Alex deserved to play any part in her son's life. She took a deep breath. He'd made a mistake, he'd lost his cool, he'd overplayed his hand by warning her. It was he who was deluding himself. He could prove nothing. She'd deny everything, and there was nothing he could do.

Ben had disappeared back into the bathroom with the empty glass, and she heard the unmistakable sound of running water. He was cleaning his teeth, she realised, and washing his face, and all without her instruction. She sank back on her pillows, her eyes filling with tears.

He was such a good little boy. Alex must be mad if he thought she'd ever give him up.

It was not until Ben emerged again, his face scrubbed and shining, and went into his room to get dressed that Sara began to suspect she had been a little naïve. And when Ben appeared again, with his boots unfastened and his shirt askew, she had some inkling of what was going on.

'I'll tell Mrs Fraser you've got a headache, shall I?' he asked brightly, edging hopefully towards the door. 'She'll probably bring you breakfast in bed. Just like Daddy used to do when we were at home.'

'Wait a minute.' Despite her discomfort, Sara managed to prop herself up on her elbows and gesture towards him. 'Come here. Your laces are unfastened. We don't want you falling down the stairs.'

Ben looked a little hesitant about approaching the bed, as if he feared that his mother might not let him go if she got her hands on him. Dear God, thought Sara weakly, was she such a possessive mother? How gratified Alex would have been to see them now.

'Come here,' she said again, trying not to lose her patience, and with a grimace at his appearance Ben obeyed.

'Hurry up,' he said. 'I don't want to be late. Uncle Alex said he might give me another lesson, if you didn't mind.'

Sara's throat tightened. But I do mind, she wanted to say fiercely. I don't want you having anything to do with your uncle Alex! But a glance at her son's face prevented her from voicing the words. She recalled the old maxim about loving someone to death, and suffocating Ben's natural spirit would achieve nothing.

'Well,' she said now as she fastened his laces, choosing her words with care, 'don't be surprised if Uncle Alex has forgotten all about it. He told me last night that he's going back to London tomorrow, and he may not have time to come over here from Ragdale today and play with you.'

Ben's face dropped. 'It's not playing, Mum!' he exclaimed defensively. 'Uncle Alex says someone like me should def'nitely be able to ride a horse.'

Sara couldn't stop herself. 'Someone like you?' she echoed.

'Yes.' Ben puffed out his chest. 'Uncle Alex says all the men in the fam'ly learn to ride when they're children. It's 'cos it's tra...tra...gel...'

'Traditional?'

'That's right.' Ben's little face beamed. 'He says I'll learn more about the 'state that way.'

'The state?'

Ben sighed. 'No, the estate,' he corrected her impatiently. 'Did you know Grandpa owns most of the land I can see from my window?'

Sara finished buttoning his shirt correctly, adjusted his V-necked sweater and sank back against the pillows. It was no good, she thought tiredly. She was too ill right now to put up a fight. Let Alex tell him what he liked. As soon as she was on her feet again they were leaving.

'So, can I go now?'

Belatedly Ben was evidently feeling some remorse, for he hovered beside the bed now instead of charging out of the door.

'Why not?' said Sara flatly, refusing to allay his fears. 'But don't tell Uncle Alex I'm not well. I'll probably be up and about when you get back.'

CHAPTER SIX

BUT Sara wasn't up and about. The headache, which had seemed to have a fairly obvious cause, developed into a fever, and Dr Lomas was called from Corbridge to diagnose that she'd caught a chill. Evidently the violent change of temperature had lowered her resistance, and in spite of her best efforts she was obliged to stay in bed.

During the following days she had unwilling cause to wish that Alex were still at Ragdale. But he'd departed at the weekend as predicted, and because the Reeds were not used to young children Ben spent a lot of his time upstairs.

In consequence Sara didn't get as much rest as she should have done, and therefore took longer than she might have to recover from the chill. Mrs Fraser did what she could, but she had her own duties to attend to, and Mrs Reed was too strict with Alison to allow her to look after the child.

'You really need a nanny,' Elizabeth Reed declared, on one of her infrequent visits to the sickroom. 'The child needs some stimulation. He shouldn't be playing up here all day.'

'There's not much point in employing a nanny when I shall be leaving for London as soon as I'm better,' replied Sara weakly. 'I'm sorry, Mrs Reed, but it's my decision.' She paused. 'Ben can come back for holidays, of course.'

'How kind.' Elizabeth's lips thinned. But then, as if thinking better of what she had been about to say, she forced a polite smile. 'But not before the new year—your leaving, I mean? Surely you'll let Ben have his first Christmas in England with his family?'

I'm his family now, protested Sara silently, disliking this persistent need to stifle how she felt. But until she could see Harry's solicitor and sort out her financial affairs there didn't seem to be a lot of point in making a fuss.

Besides, even though it caused a sinking in her stomach, Elizabeth's mention of Christmas had thrown a spanner in the works. Until then Harry's death had succeeded in masking the season, but the fact that it was barely three weeks to Christmas had to be faced.

Harry's solicitors were based in London, and although she'd already informed them of the situation they'd advised her to wait until she was in London before attempting to prove the will. There were minor details to be dealt with, and one or two bequests to discuss with her, and a codicil that needed to be defined.

As Sara hadn't known about the codicil anyway, she'd been obliged to accept their judgement, but now she wished that they'd been more forthcoming when she'd rung. After all, she knew what was in the will—she and Harry had made their wills together—and the bequests the man had mentioned concerned Ben in any case.

Still, until she felt stronger she didn't have a lot of choice. Perhaps she might manage a day in London before Christmas, and visit the solicitors' office then. Her real plans would have to wait until the new year, however. She'd prefer not to antagonise Harry's parents as well.

With this in mind she was able to offer some non-committal response that evidently satisfied her mother-in-law. And, after all, the Reeds might turn out to be allies if Alex chose to tell them what he said he knew. She couldn't believe that they'd condone his actions. Or believe him either, she assured herself with some relief. Harry had been their elder son; they'd loved him dearly. They'd never allow anything to sully his memory.

Altogether Sara was in bed for ten days, and even after she was up it took another week for her to recover sufficiently to go downstairs. Her poor appetite had contributed to her susceptibility to the chill, the doctor had said, and for a while he had feared that it might develop into pneumonia.

So, although she'd protested that she'd get fat, Mrs Fraser had insisted on her swallowing every mouthful of the soups and stews she made for her. She'd even stood over her while she'd eaten them, and there was no denying that by the time she was able to get dressed again she felt infinitely stronger.

Ben, for one, was delighted when she could get up and about. For all that she had expected Alex to return to Ragdale and take advantage of her incapacity in order to spend as much time as possible with the boy, he was still in London, and Ben's ability to entertain himself had worn very thin. In consequence he took a real delight in accompanying his mother around the gardens, and one afternoon Robert invited them to join him on a visit to his office in Corbridge.

As well as running the small estate his father had left him, Robert was also a partner in a firm of chartered surveyors located in the small town, and although he insisted that it was a modest concern their services were in demand. It wasn't far to Newcastle and the commercial needs of a large city, and Erskine and Reed were noted for their efficiency and skill.

It was the first indication Sara had had that James Erskine and her father-in-law were partners, and Robert explained that the income he received from his business affairs helped considerably with the running of the estate. 'Most of what is received in rents has to be reinvested for the future,' he explained when Sara commented that she didn't know how he found the time to do two jobs. 'Besides, I enjoy meeting other people. And surveying other people's problems instead of my own.'

'Do we have other animals as well as horses?' asked Ben suddenly from his position on the back seat of the Range Rover, and his grandfather smiled.

'Only the dogs,' he said ruefully. 'But my tenants have every kind of domestic animal. What would you like to see? Cows or sheep? Or perhaps a pig or two?'

Ben gave an excited whoop. 'All of them!' he exclaimed, frightening his grandfather's old retriever in the process. 'Oh, sit down, Nell,' he ordered. 'I wasn't talking to you.'

'I think you should calm down,' declared his mother evenly. 'It's not as if you've never seen any cows before.' She looked at Robert. 'A landowner Harry met in Rio owned a cattle ranch near São Joaquim.'

'And you visited his ranch?'

'Several times,' agreed Sara quietly. 'It wasn't far from Los Santos that Harry was killed.'

'Oh, my dear.' Robert's hand came to cover both of hers in her lap, and for a moment Sara thought that she was going to cry. She might not have loved Harry as much as he'd loved her, but she wouldn't have believed that she could miss him so much.

The visit to Corbridge was successful in two ways. In one she felt that it had enabled her and Harry's father to get to know one another better, and in another it had offered an opportunity for her to visit the shops. There was a lot that she wanted, and she knew that any serious clothes shopping would have to wait until she could go into Newcastle. But she found a small shop that sold handmade sweaters, and another in which she discovered a skirt. These, together with some warmer shirts for Ben, made her feel that she had accomplished a lot.

There was a strange car in the drive when they got back to Perry Edmunds—a sleek black Mercedes; it was parked at the side of the house. The garages were all at the back of the building, and it was possible that it belonged to Elizabeth Reed, or someone else who was just visiting.

'Ah, Alex is back,' remarked his father, thereby identifying the owner of the Mercedes. And, unaware of Sara's sudden stiffening, he went on, 'I dare say you'll be glad to see a different face.'

'Uncle Alex?' exclaimed Ben, releasing his seat belt and jogging forward in his seat. 'Is that his car? Isn't it big? Oh . . . do you think he'd take me for a ride?'

'I don't think—'

'I'm sure he would.' Robert overrode Sara's automatic denial without hesitation. 'He'll be looking forward to seeing you again. I was speaking to him on the phone last night and he asked how you both were. He's been quite concerned about you, Sara—and Ben, of course.'

'Has he?'

Ben was endearingly eager, and Sara thrust open her door in disgust. If she sat there any longer she'd say something unforgivable, and she had no wish to quarrel with Alex's father.

Alex himself appeared as she was unloading the bags containing the clothes she had bought from the back of the vehicle. In the informal attire of dark shirt and black jeans, he came down the steps to meet them, fielding Ben's excited greeting as he took the plastic carriers from her hands. 'How are you feeling?' he asked politely as she surrendered her belongings. 'I must say you've got a little more colour in your cheeks.'

'Than when?' asked Sara tersely, marshalling her nerves to face him. If he intended to bring up that encounter in his sitting room, she felt more than prepared to fight her corner.

'Than the morning I left,' returned Alex lightly, leaving her with wide eyes and jaw sagging. 'I called to see my mother and father before I left, and I looked in on you, but you were asleep.' His eyes mocked her. 'But not any more, eh?'

'Did you get back today?'

Robert's casual enquiry diverted his son, and with Ben clinging to Alex's legs the two men started for the house. But they paused at the foot of the steps for Sara to catch up with them, and she hurried somewhat inelegantly indoors.

Tea was being served in the sitting room, and although Sara would have preferred to go upstairs and compose herself Ben's presence made any chance of escape impossible. 'Oh, muffins!' he exclaimed, smelling the toasted, flat buns as soon as he came in the door. In a very short time he had adapted to English eating habits, and Sara guessed that she had Mrs Fraser to thank—or otherwise—for that.

'Your father always loved having muffins for tea,' remarked Robert, with a rallying glance in Sara's direction. But Elizabeth protested that it had been Alex who'd liked them best, and that Harry had preferred scones with jam and cream.

Sara managed not to look at Alex during this exchange, shedding her warm overcoat and moving nervously towards the fire. The one advantage of Perry Edmunds was its proximity to Edmundsfield Forest, and even on her first visit she had enjoyed warming herself at a real log fire.

Ben was edging towards the tea-tray where the plate of muffins was waiting, but his grandmother directed him to go and wash his hands. 'But why do I have to wash my hands?' he protested. 'Mum and Grandpa have been out too. They're not dirty. Look! I've just been sitting in the car.'

'Are you arguing with me, Ben?' enquired his grandmother sharply. And then she added, 'And how many times must I tell you that it's Grandpapa, not Grandpa? Now, you either hurry along and do as you're told or you won't get any muffins. You're a very impertinent little boy and someone should take you in hand.'

Sara's absorption in the open fire fled. 'Ben isn't—' she began, but before she could get any further Alex's voice drowned her words.

'I don't think that was an unreasonable question, Mother,' he declared, earning an exasperated glance from his parent. He turned to the little boy, who was looking half-tearful now. 'You've been stroking Nell, haven't you, Ben? Now, you don't want her hairs on your muffin, do you?'

Ben shook his head. Sara could see that he was trying hard to hold back his tears, but there were evident signs of distress in the way he kept rubbing his nose. 'I'll come with you, Ben,' she said, starting back across the thickly patterned carpet, but Alex was already leading him out of the door, and she came to an awkward halt.

'Alex will see he comes to no harm,' her father-in-law put in comfortingly, and Sara was obliged to resume her place by the fire.

'Alex takes too much upon himself,' remarked Elizabeth tersely, and for once Sara seconded her mother-in-law's opinion wholeheartedly. 'And while you're here, Sara,' she added, instantly shattering their harmony, 'I've invited Christine Graham to come and see you tomorrow.'

Sara frowned. 'Christine Graham?'

'Yes.' Elizabeth chose not to look at her as she spoke, making a play of stirring the teapot and adjusting the cups in their saucers. 'She's Angus Graham's daughter—

one of Robert's tenants. And as she's just finished with
the Armstrongs I thought the timing was quite ideal.'

'Timing?'

Sara was still totally confused, though she was sure
that the apprehension she was feeling was not misplaced. 'She was Pamela Armstrong's nanny,' said
Robert shortly, growing tired of his wife's prevarication.
'Elizabeth thought you might welcome her assistance—
so long as you're here with us.'

Sara swallowed. 'A nanny?'

'Yes, a nanny,' said her mother-in-law defensively.
'You must admit that Ben has been running wild. He
needs discipline; he needs elementary education. Both
Harry and Alex could read at his age, and do simple
arithmetic as well.'

Sara had never felt so angry—or so frustrated. 'Don't
you think I should have been consulted,' she exclaimed,
'before you invited some strange woman to look after
Ben?'

'You are being consulted,' retorted Elizabeth impatiently. 'If you don't like the girl then we'll have to
think of something else. But don't dismiss the idea just
because I—we—suggested it. You have to admit you've
been in no state to look after Ben yourself.'

'I've been ill—'

'I know that. And I'm sure in the normal way you
devote a generous portion of your time to the boy, and
I've no argument with the way he behaves—well, not
usually anyway. But a mother's love is not sufficient.
An intelligent child needs challenges, and I don't think
Ben is being stretched.'

'He's four—'

'He'll soon be five,' replied Elizabeth inflexibly. 'We're
all agreed that it's time he started to learn, and I have
it on good authority that Christine is an excellent nanny.

She's been with the Armstrongs seven years, since their youngest child was born.'

'Seven years,' said Sara, feeling nauseous.

'The Armstrongs are leaving the country, and Christine prefers to stay in England,' Robert took it upon himself to explain.

'Not just in England,' his wife pointed out swiftly, 'but in Northumberland. She has elderly parents living in Hexham. It wouldn't be fair for her to abandon them, not as they're getting old.'

Sara was silent. It seemed that whichever way she turned the Reeds were there to thwart her. Both Elizabeth and Robert Reed knew that she didn't want to stay in Edmundsfield, and Alex was doubly cognisant of her desire to get away.

'It will be your decision,' her father-in-law assured her as Alex and her son came back into the room. Ben was looking infinitely more cheerful now, his earlier rebuke quite forgotten, and he came to perch on the arm of his mother's chair, his endearing grin firmly in place. But Sara found it difficult to respond to him, despite what his grandfather had said. She had the feeling that her son might prove the biggest stumbling block of all.

For the remainder of the day Sara managed to avoid any private conversation with Alex. Of course, the fact that he left after taking tea with them made it easier, though the idea of him living alone at Ragdale caught at her throat.

Her mother-in-law solved that particular problem for her, however. She announced at supper that Alex was dining with the Erskines instead. Apparently James Erskine wanted some advice on a legal matter that he hoped Alex might be able to help him with. 'You'll know that Alex trained as a barrister before he decided to take up journalism,' she said casually. 'Perhaps now he'll consider entering the Bar again.'

Sara offered some innocuous rejoinder. England was big enough for both of them, she told herself. Besides, if Alex remained at Ragdale he'd soon get tired of baiting her. Whatever he said, that incident five years ago was a part of the past, not the future.

All the same, as she lay in bed that night she found herself remembering how she'd felt when she'd first discovered that she was pregnant. She had been married to Harry by then, of course, and he'd had no reason to doubt that Ben was his son. On the one occasion when she'd tried to explain what had happened he'd changed the subject. It was as if he subconsciously hadn't wanted to know the truth.

And, she recalled, she had spent the last five years trying to convince herself that she had been mistaken. Babies did sometimes come early—particularly babies that were larger than the norm. Ben could be Harry's child; she could have conceived a whole month before the wedding. They had been living together, for heaven's sake. For almost a year...

The trouble was that she didn't believe it. No matter what she did, she couldn't escape her fears. Ben was Alex's child, she knew it with a feeling that was almost visceral. Those weeks she'd spent at Perry Edmunds had ruined her life.

Of course, to begin with, it had been the memory of what had happened between her and Alex that had tortured her constantly. She and Harry had married just a few days after her return to London, and then honeymooned off the Ionian coast of Greece, and she'd lived in denial the whole time. It couldn't have happened, she'd told herself; she must have dreamed it. But the dream had become a nightmare with incredible speed, and then there'd been no way out.

The irony had been Harry's reaction to her pregnancy. Her half-guilty admission of her condition had met with only exuberance and joy. Her attempt to cast any doubt on his rejoicing had been quickly deflected. When Ben had been born in Kuwait some six months later Harry had insisted on being there.

And he'd been there ever since, Sara acknowledged now, feeling the familiar prick of tears behind her eyes. Obviously so long as his brother had been alive Alex had been prepared to bide his time. He might not even have suspected until he'd seen Ben. But her apprehensions had been more than warranted, it seemed.

She'd certainly never dreamed that Alex might confront her with his suspicions, for all that. And that was all they were, she told herself fiercely. He could hardly prove that Ben was his. Her wisest course was to ride the storm. So long as she kept her head, he was powerless. There was no way that he'd get a confession out of her.

And, so far as Ben was concerned, spending time with his uncle needn't be a bad thing. The little boy had just lost his father, after all, and if Alex's attentions helped to ease him through that traumatic event then what had she to lose? The last thing she wanted was to alienate her son by being too aggressive. Until Christmas was over she could afford to be generous, she decided. By constantly fighting with Alex she was playing into his hands.

So the following morning, when Ben came bouncing into the bedroom as Sara was drinking the early-morning tea that Mrs Fraser had brought her and asked if he might have another riding lesson with Alex, she didn't demur. 'Why not?' she asked, earning a little whoop of excitement. 'So long as Uncle Alex doesn't mind. But don't be surprised if he doesn't come over. He may have other things to do.'

'He doesn't!' exclaimed Ben confidently, jogging about on the end of the bed. 'He said he'd come over last night.'

'Last night?' Sara frowned, and, putting the cup aside, levered herself more comfortably against the pillows.

'When Grandmama grumbled about me washing my hands,' explained Ben patiently. 'When we got back from that ride with Grandpa—Grandpapa!' He grimaced. 'Why can't I just say Grandpa? That's what Daddy always said.'

'Yes, well . . .' Sara was endeavouring not to allow the instinctive resentment she felt at Alex's appropriation of her son yet again to surface.

It was all very well granting him certain rights where Ben was concerned when she could choose what those rights should be. But his indifference to her feelings was wearing, to say the least. His lip-service to the formalities didn't wash with her at all. He was consistently undermining her authority by encouraging her son to challenge her wishes. 'You can't always get what you want,' she finished crisply, not unaware of the ramifications of that statement—for both of them.

'But I can go out with Uncle Alex? You're not going to change your mind?'

'Of course not,' said Sara, though it was through her teeth. 'Now, go and get your wash.'

While Sara had been ill Ben had taken to having his breakfast upstairs with her, but for the past few days both of them had eaten the meal in the small morning room. This morning, however, Sara half wished that she could revert to their previous arrangement. The thought of maybe confronting Alex before she'd eaten was more daunting than she cared to admit.

But there was no way she could confide that to Ben, and after a swift shower—during which time her son fretted anxiously that he was going to be late—she dressed and went downstairs, aware of a certain breathless anxiety as they reached the gloomy confines of the hall.

Her tension proved unnecessary, however. When Mrs Fraser detected their presence and came to enquire what they would like to eat she was quick to tell Ben that his uncle was already down at the stable yard. 'He had a bowl of porridge here an hour ago, and I dare say he and Darcy have cleaned out half a dozen stalls by now. But don't worry, little man. He said to tell you where he was.'

Ben's face beamed, and he turned to his mother with glowing eyes. 'Did you hear that, Mum? Uncle Alex is waiting for me. Can I do without any toast this morning?'

Sara looked at Mrs Fraser. 'Alex had porridge, you say?'

'That's right, Mrs Reed. I always say you won't go far wrong with a bowl of my oatmeal under your belt. Alex doesn't feed himself properly over at Ragdale. I always have something ready for him here.'

'Then we'll have porridge too,' declared Sara, gambling that Ben wouldn't object to copying his idol. 'And tea, I think, for Ben. But could I have coffee as usual?'

Ben's small mouth compressed, but he evidently knew better than to push his luck, and Mrs Fraser earned his undying gratitude by bringing the porridge back in double-quick time. Sara, who had been used to having toast, occasionally with an egg or a piece of bacon, if the housekeeper could persuade her, was surprised to find that she enjoyed the oatmeal too, especially as it was served with cream.

'Can I go now?' Ben asked after scraping his dish clean and gulping down a cup of tea. And although Sara could have wished for longer with her son she managed an assenting nod.

But then, just as Ben was dashing out of the door, she stopped him. 'I—wait a minute,' she said, emptying her own cup. 'I'll come with you. Just as far as the stables,' she amended, seeing the doubt in Ben's small face. 'I feel like some fresh air. And it is a lovely crisp morning.'

'Well, you won't be long, will you—getting ready, I mean?' Ben asked anxiously. 'I've only got to put my coat on. You can't go out like that.'

'Like what?' Sara looked down at her bronze silk blouse, teamed with the almost ankle-length woollen skirt that she'd bought the day before, and grimaced. 'Don't I look smart enough for you? I thought you liked this colour.'

'It's your shoes,' said Ben impatiently, eyeing her low-heeled pumps with a critical eye. 'You need boots in the stable yard. Everybody knows that.'

'Then I'll borrow a pair of Grandmama's wellingtons,' said Sara tolerantly, remembering that she had seen some standing by the garden door. And her mother-in-law's waxed jacket, too, she thought, helping Ben into his parka. Elizabeth need never know.

All the same, as she pushed her stockinged feet into the cold rubber boots she wondered why she was putting herself through this. Her decision at the breakfast table to put her ideas of the night before into practice didn't seem so urgent now. Treating Alex with civility would be difficult enough, without rushing headlong into a confrontation. Still, the sooner she proved to him that his persistent baiting wasn't going to work, the sooner she could get on with her life...

CHAPTER SEVEN

OUTSIDE, the air was crisp and cold. Although the elms and rowan trees that grew around the gravelled courtyard were bare now, the sun gave even their skeletal limbs some beauty, creating a tracery of webbing against the sky. Fortunately many of the trees were conifers, whose needles sparkled with the overnight frost. Like Christmas trees, thought Sara fancifully, wondering what Ben would think when he saw his first fall of snow.

The back of the house formed one side of a courtyard, with the garages and the block of outhouses creating an L-shaped barrier on one side, the wall of the kitchen garden towering importantly on the other. In summer the garden wall was almost hidden beneath a mass of wild roses, while the garages sported rambling wisteria along their eaves.

Between the garages and the kitchen garden a pathway led down to the stables. At present the footway was carpeted with rotting leaves, but the frost had given a crunchy substance to the mulch. Even so, it was still quite slippy, and Sara was glad that she hadn't ventured out in her shoes.

The stables at Perry Edmunds were set on two sides of a square exercise area. Although Harry hadn't been much interested in horses, Alex had brought her down here a couple of times to give her a glimpse of his father's hunters. Only it had been summer then, and most of the animals had been out in the paddocks. This morning the half-dozen or so horses in residence were more easily identified, peering over the half-doors of their stalls.

Except for the one that Alex was grooming, Sara saw, her nerves stiffening automatically at the sight of her brother-in-law. Despite the cold morning, he was working with his shirtsleeves rolled back, his breath condensing into a mist in the freezing air.

Whether he had heard their approach or not, he didn't look in their direction until Ben shouted, 'Uncle Alex! Uncle Alex! I'm here!' Only then did he appear to notice that the boy had brought his mother, and he straightened from brushing the mare's coat to give Sara a polite nod.

'Good morning.'

'Good morning,' said Sara carefully. 'I hope you don't mind; I thought I'd renew my acquaintance with the estate.'

'Why should I mind?' responded Alex. 'I just didn't think horses were your forte.'

Was that a criticism? Sara wasn't sure, but, suppressing an instinctive urge to retaliate, she forced a smile. 'That's the trouble, Alex. You don't know anything about me. I thought you'd remember—I like horses. I just never had the chance to learn to ride.'

'Is that an invitation to me to offer to teach you?' enquired Alex drily. 'Don't you trust me to look after Ben myself? Or are you afraid of what we might talk about when you're not around?'

That was definitely a criticism, thought Sara impatiently. And joining them on their rides hadn't even occurred to her. It seemed that Alex was as suspicious of her as she was of him.

Ben, meanwhile, was getting restless. He didn't understand most of what they were talking about, but the suggestion that his mother might want to learn to ride was too dismaying to miss. 'She doesn't want to learn to ride!' he exclaimed. 'She's far too old for lessons! That's right, Mum, isn't it? You're going back now—back to the house.' His eyes were wide, and he gazed at her imploringly. 'You don't really want to stay with us.'

Sara shook her head, viewing her son's anxious face with wry amusement. It was hard to get cross with Ben, even if he was making her feel like the skeleton at the feast. And she could hardly blame Alex for her son's behaviour. She could tell from Ben's uneasy stance that he was afraid of what his uncle might say.

'No,' she said at last, and saw the relief in his eyes and realising in any case that she didn't have a choice. To begin with, she was hardly dressed to mount a horse, and besides, the cold was definitely beginning to bite. 'I'll see you later,' she added, pushing her hands deep into the pockets of Elizabeth's jacket. And then she added to Alex, though without censure, 'Don't keep him out too long.'

'I won't.'

Alex had begun rolling down the sleeves of his shirt as he'd spoken, and Sara suddenly saw the dark brown cashmere jacket that had been tossed carelessly over the fence. As he pulled it on she found herself noticing the hard muscles of his arms, and the way his narrow trousers fitted so snugly about his sex...

Oh, God!

Horror-stricken, she turned away before he observed the raw awareness in her face. In heaven's name, it was years since she had looked at any man other than her husband, and the fact that it was this man turned her stomach.

'I'll walk you back.'

To her dismay he was beside her now, buttoning his jacket over his flat stomach then adjusting his watch, which had become loose about his wrist. His scent, his smell, even the sight of the dark hairs emerging from his cuff disturbed her, and she had to steel herself to meet his enquiring gaze.

'That won't be necessary,' she said, keeping her voice civil only with an effort, and earning herself a look of gratitude from her son. 'I—' She broke off. 'I'm in no hurry. I thought I might go back...that way, instead.'

She pointed somewhat vaguely in the direction of the shrubbery that she believed flanked the private gardens of the house, and Alex regarded her with some amusement in his eyes. 'That's the cesspit,' he remarked. 'I didn't know you were interested in sewage. There's a farm over the other side of the village that you might find fascinating if that's so.'

Sara pressed her lips together, realising two things all at once that gave her pause. The first was that she'd forgotten that Alex had a sense of humour, and the second was how dangerous that could be.

'Oh, I—'

Desperately seeking something to say to regain her composure, Sara cast her eyes wildly around the yard. There had to be another way back to the house, but her knowledge of the area was badly flawed.

'I think it would be wiser if you went straight back along the path,' Alex volunteered now, and she remembered how gentle he could be. Subconsciously she'd been aware of this in all their altercations, which was another reason why she'd chosen to keep him at arm's length.

That, and the very real threat he represented, she acknowledged uneasily, wondering if it wouldn't just be easier to remain enemies. Being civil only threw up different problems, not least the fact that she wasn't as indifferent to his dark attraction as she'd believed.

'I—perhaps so,' she said, hoping that he would take this as a dismissal, but to her dismay he fell in at her side. Ignoring Ben's snort of outrage, he accompanied her back along the path, and Sara trod with extra care as they returned.

It wouldn't do for her to fall, she thought a little dizzily. She had no wish for Alex to grab her arm. While his saving her from falling might be all very well in a novel, she was desperate not to feel his hands upon her.

Or, more accurately, for him not to sense any response to his touch, she admitted, with a sideways glance. How could she have deluded herself that Alex wasn't a sexual animal? Or that she had buried all emotion with her husband?

Thankfully it took only a few minutes to reach the back of the house, and Sara picked up a little speed across the cobbled yard. Even so, Alex stayed with her until she reached the garden door, leaning past her to open it with studied ease.

'OK?' he asked, and she bobbed her head.

'Thank you.'

'I take it we've called a truce,' he added. 'Am I right?'

Sara bit her lip. 'I don't know what you mean,' she protested. 'Just because we've had our differences...doesn't mean we...can't behave politely with one another, does it?'

Alex's mouth twitched. 'That's not exactly what you were saying a couple of weeks ago,' he pointed out. 'But if you've had a change of heart who am I to object?'

Sara held up her head. 'I just think life's too short to sustain squalid little quarrels,' she declared with apparent coolness, though her nails were digging into her palms. 'I don't want to fall out with you, Alex. You are Ben's uncle, after all.'

His eyes darkened at this, but the awareness of Ben, pulling at his sleeve, prevented him from saying anything more. One to me, I think, thought Sara smugly, stepping through the garden door. From the ashes of defeat she'd snatched a victory.

*   *   *

To her surprise, Mrs Fraser informed her that Elizabeth Reed was waiting for her in the library. As her mother-in-law wasn't usually an early riser, Sara viewed this development rather apprehensively, though she knew better than to ask the housekeeper what was going on.

In consequence she was forced to shed her coat and boots and go immediately to find her, forgoing the cup of coffee she'd been looking forward to having in the kitchen. In recent days, after she and Ben had been walking they'd usually joined Mrs Fraser and Alison for a hot drink upon returning. It was a nuisance to be summoned in this way.

Elizabeth wasn't dressed. A warm velvet housecoat in a rather attractive shade of green prevented her from feeling any chill—unlike Sara, who found the library less than hospitable, with draughts you didn't feel when the curtains were drawn.

'Ah, Sara!' exclaimed her mother-in-law from her position in an armchair beside the struggling fire. Clearly the logs were damp and weren't responding but merely creating a lot of smoke. 'I'm so glad you're back. Christine will be here in half an hour.'

'Christine?'

For a moment Sara couldn't think who Elizabeth was talking about, and the other woman made a resigned face.

'The prospective nanny,' she prompted irritably. 'Don't say you've forgotten. Christine Graham. I mentioned that she was coming yesterday afternoon.'

'Oh, yes.' Sara knew an overwhelming sense of weariness. Were she and Ben never to be allowed to please themselves? Yet that wasn't really fair, she thought. Ben seemed to be enjoying himself. It was she who was bearing the burden of Harry's death.

'Yes,' agreed her mother-in-law. 'I've asked her to come at ten o'clock, and Robert says I should let you

interview her yourself. I just wanted to remind you that
I expect you to employ her. We—that is, the family—
will take care of her salary, of course.'

Sara drew a breath. 'That's not necessary,' she said,
mentally calculating how much a professional nanny
might charge. She had a little money, but not enough
to employ staff on a permanent basis. Still, this was only
a temporary arrangement, after all.

'We insist,' said Elizabeth glacially. 'I'm well aware
that Harry wasn't a rich man when he died. And the
circumstances of—well, of his death may nullify his insurance. Of course, Harry may have allowed for that,
but until his will is proved we can't know for certain.
And Robert and I would like to do this for you—for
Ben. He is our only grandchild, isn't he?'

Sara felt a hint of colour invade her neck. 'As far as
I know,' she responded half-flippantly, and then, realising she was letting her nerves get the better of her, she
shook her head. 'It's very kind of you, of course. And
don't think I don't appreciate it, but—'

'That's settled, then,' said Elizabeth. 'I'll go and get
dressed.'

There was no point in arguing. So long as she was
living in this house with these people, Sara realised, she
had little choice but to do as she was told. Besides, it
wasn't that important. She might not even like the nanny.
And she was not going to leave Ben with some woman
she actively disliked.

She was considering going upstairs to put on some
make-up when Alison appeared in the doorway.
'Christine's here, Mrs Reed. She says she's a few minutes
early. Shall I put her in the sitting room or show her
in?'

Sara caught her breath, her hand going automatically
to her hair. Fortunately the silky bob hadn't been affected by the weather, and it wasn't as if she wanted to
impress anyone.

'Mmm—oh, show her in, please,' she invited now. 'And perhaps you could bring us some coffee?'

'No problem,' replied Alison cheerfully. And, turning, she said, 'It's all right, Chris. Mrs Reed says you can come in.'

Christine Graham was nothing like Sara had expected. Round, and not very tall, she had the comfortable demeanour of a countrywoman, with the kind of homely features no anxious employer need fear. She was nothing like the girls in Rio, many of whom had been scarcely out of their teens, or the glamorous au pair her boss had employed in London.

Her smile was friendly, and after Sara had shaken hands and invited her to take a seat it was no effort to remark on her evident familiarity with Alison.

'We went to school together,' said Christine simply. 'We've known one another for years. Only, when Alison left to get married I went to university.'

Sara nodded. 'Really?' She grimaced. 'I didn't realise it was necessary to get a degree to look after children.'

'It isn't.' Christine explained, 'Initially I'd planned to study child psychology, but it didn't take me long to realise that I enjoyed the practical side of the course much more than the academic. In any case, in my final year I left and entered a nursery training course in Newcastle. Since then I've had two jobs, and I've got references from both. My last employer is leaving the country, but I didn't want to go.'

'Yes, my mother-in-law mentioned something about that.' Sara bit her lip thoughtfully. 'This...might be just a temporary post, you understand? I'm hoping to move south in the spring.'

In the spring!

Sara wondered where that decision had come from, and chided herself for not telling the young woman exactly what she intended. A few weeks after Christmas was hardly the spring, and she wouldn't want her to lose some other position because of her.

But Christine had already acknowledged that she knew there was some doubt about the length of time that her services would be required, and she didn't mind. 'My parents live in Hexham,' she explained. 'And as my brother lives in Canada I feel as if they're my responsibility. My mother has angina, you see, and she can't do very much for herself.'

'I'm sorry.' Sara found herself liking Christine more and more, and by the time Alison came back with the tray of coffee they were chatting about Ben as if they were old friends. Christine had also confessed that she'd been married once, but the relationship had foundered. The child she had been carrying at the time had been stillborn, and she'd consoled herself by looking after other people's children ever since.

Only Elizabeth's reappearance cast a certain shadow over the proceedings. Clearly she had not expected her daughter-in-law and the nanny to hit it off so well. If Sara wasn't mistaken, she thought the older woman was disappointed. She had evidently expected to have to force the issue once again.

It was eventually agreed that Christine would come again the following morning. Because she was between jobs at the moment she had no other commitments, and she was eager to meet her charge. Ben and Alex hadn't got back by the time she was leaving, and Sara assured her that the omission would be rectified the following day.

'I gather you approve,' remarked Elizabeth tersely when Sara returned to the library after seeing Christine out. 'One word—I wouldn't advise you to get too familiar. Miss Graham is an employee, not a friend.'

'Perhaps I find friends are in short supply at Perry Edmunds,' replied Sara shortly. 'And we did have people who worked for us in Rio, you know. Just because I find *Christine* sympathetic doesn't mean I intend to make an ally of her.'

'An ally!' Elizabeth's narrow brows arched in some disdain. 'My child, I wasn't suggesting anything so dramatic. You really must remember we're your family now.'

Sara made no direct response to this, only excused herself soon after and left the room. Let her mother-in-law think what she liked; the Reeds were not her family, she thought defensively. She refused to accept that her name was Reed as well.

Notwithstanding the misgivings she had had about employing a nanny, in the days that followed Sara had reason to be grateful for the freedom it granted her. Since Harry's death she hadn't realised what a weight the responsibility for Ben had put upon her, but with Christine's arrival she found time to be herself.

It helped enormously that Ben liked the other woman. Oh, there had been one or two tantrums when he'd discovered that the lessons he was expected to share with the nanny encroached on the time he wanted to spend with Alex, but Sara had been firm. There'd be plenty of time to spend with his uncle at weekends, she'd informed him, allaying any twinge of conscience by reminding herself that she hadn't made the arrangements, her mother-in-law had.

In any case, as if to confound her totally, Alex often came over to his parents' house in the late afternoon or early evening after that. He'd occasionally join his mother for afternoon tea, when he knew that Ben was likely to be present, and in consequence, whenever Sara knew he was coming, she endeavoured to be absent. The fact that Robert Reed had put a car at her disposal was a definite advantage on these occasions.

Because of family ties Christine had chosen not to live in. She arrived at Perry Edmunds at about eight-thirty in the morning, and then left for home again around half past four. There were no hard and fast rules to her timekeeping. If Sara had asked her to come earlier or stay later she would have. But with Mrs Fraser living in the house her services were not required for babysitting, and Sara was never out beyond the time when her in-laws had tea.

This meant that Sara retained the right to bathe her son and put him to bed without creating any divided loyalties, and at weekends, when Christine didn't come at all, their time was their own.

Of course, Ben spent most weekend mornings down at the stables, and it was only a matter of time before Alex suggested that he might take her son to Ragdale for the afternoon.

He broached the subject with Sara about a week before Christmas, when she returned from town rather earlier than was usual and encountered him in her mother-in-law's sitting room. She'd been to Newcastle, ostensibly to do some Christmas shopping, but in reality she had spent most of the afternoon sitting over a coffee in a department-store café.

It was foolish avoiding him, she knew, and hardly in keeping with her intention to treat him casually. And, to be honest, she wondered sometimes if she was afraid of him. But since that morning when she'd accompanied Ben down to the stables she'd ensured that they'd never been alone.

And the sight of Alex's car in the driveway had elicited very uneasy emotions, the stronger of which was the urge to turn and run. But on this occasion Robert's car, following hers into the driveway, had forestalled any such madness, and she'd been forced to drive into the garage, where the small Renault was most usually parked.

Besides, she'd assured herself firmly, it was only a few more days to Christmas. As soon as the festive season was over she could start planning her escape. It wasn't as if any of them was feeling particularly festive. If it hadn't been for Ben, Sara had thought, she might have forgone the celebrations this year.

It had been easier to walk into Elizabeth Reed's sitting room with Robert at her side. All the same, the sight of Alex, lying flat on his back on the floor wrestling with her son, brought a hot stain of colour to her cheeks. She hadn't realised how intimate they had become, and the suspicion that she and Ben were drifting apart gripped her stomach with a surge of panic.

Alex saw her first. Perhaps he had detected the sound of footsteps in the hall, which explained the guarded expression on his face. In any event he turned his head as they walked in the door, and her eyes went directly to his.

Ben wasn't immediately aware of her arrival. He was sitting astride his uncle, pummelling Alex's chest with his fists. 'D'you give in?' he was demanding, his voice rising with childish glee, and his grandmother uttered an impatient remonstrance as his heels caught the fringe of the Turkish rug.

'I give in,' agreed Alex obediently, withdrawing his dark gaze from Sara's, and, sitting up, he lifted the boy effortlessly aside. 'Here's your mummy,' he added, drawing up one black-clad leg and pushing back the tumbled weight of his hair. 'How are you, Sara? I haven't seen you for a while. Anyone would think you were avoiding me.'

'Oh, no, I—'

Sara's instinctive denial was swiftly overridden by her son. 'You didn't give in,' he muttered, looking indignantly at his uncle. 'You said you couldn't get up, but you could!'

'Don't be silly, Ben,' said his grandmother crisply. 'And you interrupted your mother, too. That isn't polite. I see I shall have to have a word with Miss Graham. It's obvious she's not keeping her promise to improve your manners.'

'It's not important,' began Sara, more than grateful to her son for saving her from making some inane apology that she didn't mean, and Elizabeth Reed frowned.

'It is important. Ben's old enough to understand—'

'Leave it!' Alex's unexpected intervention silenced his mother, and for a few moments nobody said a word. Even his father seemed startled, his lined face hollowing accordingly, and Alex used the pregnant interval to get to his feet.

Sara wanted to look anywhere rather than at him, but her eyes were uneasily drawn to his lean frame. He'd lost weight, she thought disbelievingly as he pushed his shirt further into his trousers. He definitely looked more gaunt than he had when he'd arrived back from Kashmir.

'Tea, Sara?' he offered after a moment, breaking the uneasy quiet, and his mother seemed to gather herself as he spoke.

'I—thank you,' said Sara awkwardly, wishing that she were not a party to this fiasco, and Ben took the opportunity to seek her protection.

'Did you get me anything?' he asked, trying to peer into the carrier bag she was carrying, but before his mother could answer his grandmother suggested that Sara should take a seat.

'Is it still raining?' she asked as she poured tea into one of the bone-china cups, and the ensuing conversation robbed the moment of any lingering embarrassment.

'Not at the moment,' her husband answered, helping Sara off with her coat before joining her on one of the striped settees. 'But it's cold enough for snow. Don't you think so, Alex? Or have you spent the whole afternoon in front of the fire?'

'Not the whole afternoon,' said Alex evenly, moving to stand before the hearth. He looked down at Ben. 'I just came over fifteen minutes ago.'

'He was going to ask if you'd let me go to his house tomorrow,' mumbled the boy against Sara's shoulder. He was draped over the arm of her chair so neither of his grandparents could hear what he said. 'But I don't know if I want to go now.'

Sara put down the cup of tea that Elizabeth had just given her and strove for calm. It didn't matter that Ben's reaction to the invitation was lukewarm; the fact that it had been voiced at all filled her with indignation. Alex should have spoken to her before bringing it up with her son. She could have vetoed it then without Ben knowing anything about it.

Which, of course, had been Alex's idea, she acknowledged grimly. This kind of guerilla warfare was always so much more successful than hand-to-hand combat. By striking at her behind her back, he had successfully undermined any objection she might try to make.

And, despite Ben's sulky expression, she suspected that he did really want to go—or had done until his grandmother had reproved him. Naturally he would turn to her if he felt threatened from another source, but how long would that last if Alex provided an alternative and, perhaps, more sympathetic ear?

'I thought you might like to join us, Sara,' the object of her recriminations remarked now, revealing that his hearing was remarkably acute, and Elizabeth Reed looked at her son with puzzled eyes.

'Sara has joined us,' she pointed out tersely, her tone a reminder that she hadn't forgiven him for rebuking her earlier, and Alex's mouth took on an ironic slant.

'So she has,' he observed mildly, but there was no mistaking the tolerance in his voice. 'However, I was referring to Ben's remark about going to Ragdale. If it's fine tomorrow afternoon—as it's Saturday—would that seem appropriate?'

'Well, really, I'm not sure that taking Sara to your—er—bachelor establishment would seem to be quite... discreet,' declared his mother, glancing at her husband. 'What do you think, Rob?'

'What Dad thinks isn't really relevant,' retorted Alex shortly, and Sara had the rather pleasant experience of seeing his frustration for once. Their disagreement also gave her a few welcome moments to compose her own reply, so that when he turned to her again she was ready.

'I think your mother's right,' she said, with just the right amount of reluctance in her tone. 'Maybe if I come back next year...'

'Come back?' Alex fairly snapped out the words, and for a chilling moment Sara was half-afraid that he was going to spell out his objections. But then, as if recalling where he was, and who was listening, he forced a short, mirthless laugh. 'Oh, I think we can dismiss any fears on that score,' he essayed smoothly. 'It's not as if we won't have a chaperon, is it? What do you say, Ben?'

Ben, who had been squirming around the back of Sara's chair all the while they had been talking, now fixed his uncle with a resentful stare. 'You said if Mum didn't want to go we'd go on our own,' he said gruffly, leaving Sara in no doubt that he'd prefer it that way. 'But I don't know if I want to see some stuffy old house.'

'Ben!'

Once again, Elizabeth looked rebukingly at her grandson, and as if it was all too much for him Ben wrenched himself away from his mother and ran unheedingly out of the room.

'Ben!'

This time it was Sara who spoke, but when she would have risen to go after him Robert caught her arm.

'Let him go,' he advised gently. 'I think Ben's finding it just as hard as the rest of us to come to terms with his father's death, and if he appears to behave a little selfishly at times that's only to be expected.'

'All the same, Robert—'

His wife was clearly not prepared to dismiss Ben's behaviour so easily, and once again Alex came to the boy's defence. 'He's confused,' he said flatly. 'He's been forced to adapt to a whole new way of life, a whole new country, and no sooner has he settled down here than Sara is talking of uprooting him again and taking him to London, a place as alien to him as another planet!'

Sara caught her breath. '*This* place is alien to him.'

'No, it's not.' Alex was adamant, and this time she sensed that he had both his parents' support. 'This is—*was*—his father's home. He can identify with things here, with people who remember his father as a young child. That means a lot to a boy. I know. If anyone's an alien here it's you, Sara. So don't pretend you're thinking of Ben when you talk about moving to London. Make no mistake, he belongs here.'

Sara's face burned. 'You would say that!' she exclaimed tremulously, and for a moment her eyes locked on the cold determination of his.

'Yes, I would,' he agreed harshly. 'I think you ought to think long and hard before you consider taking him away from the people who *really* have his welfare at heart!'

CHAPTER EIGHT

SARA stood stiffly at Alex's sitting-room window and watched as he and her son played an impromptu game of tag among the boxwood hedges that bisected Ragdale's sprawling gardens. It had snowed overnight, and Ben's new chunky parka was smudged with some of the powdery flakes he'd acquired during the snow fight they'd had earlier.

Alex had expected her to join them, of course. He had been unfailingly polite ever since she had telephoned him that morning to say that she would be accompanying Ben that afternoon. But, in spite of her reluctance to remain in the house that had such unpleasant memories for her, Sara was unwilling to spend any more time in his company than was absolutely necessary. Besides, the idea of dashing about in the rapidly melting slush was decidedly unattractive, and, ridiculous as the word might sound, she felt she had to retain her 'dignity' at all costs.

All the same, from her position behind the curtains she had felt a distinct pang when Alex had produced an old sledge and proceeded to show her son the delights of skidding across the sloping lawns at high speed. The knowledge that the sledge had probably been Harry's before it was Alex's was little compensation. It should have been Harry teaching Ben the fun of playing in the snow, not a man who by his own admission was ashamed of the child's conception.

Still, Ben was not to know that, and there was no doubt that the unaccustomed activity had brought some healthy colour to his rather pale cheeks. Like her, he was suffering the effects of the cooler climate, and the tans which they had once taken for granted had all but disappeared.

Even so, Sara was growing impatient with her own company, and with the awareness that by hiding behind the curtains she was tacitly acknowledging her curiosity about Alex and her son. The sitting room was warm and comfortable; there were books on the shelves and magazines on the low table; she should have seated herself beside the fire and put all thoughts of the man and the boy out of her mind.

But how could she do that in this house, with the memory of what had happened here still vividly imprinted on her mind? She had thought she'd put the actual incident behind her, but she'd realised how false that was the minute she'd stepped over the threshold. She remembered everything about this place, not least the stained-glass window on the landing. It had been the window that had beckoned her upstairs, and given Alex the opportunity he'd been looking for...

But she wouldn't think of that now, she chided herself fiercely. If Alex could invite her here without feeling any sense of remorse, why should she expand his already inflated ego by showing her real feelings? A house was just a house, for God's sake! It was the people in it who gave it its identity. And there was no doubt that it looked vastly different these days from the way it had done when the previous owners had moved out.

Of course, she hadn't seen what it was like upstairs, but the hall and this room had been improved enormously. Gone was all the Gregorys' old furniture and worn carpets, and in their place were elegant, polished pieces with delicate veneers. Like the suite of rooms at his father's house, the walls here were hung with pale silk, and although the curtains were velvet they were in a warm shade of ruby.

Sara's feet sank into the rich Persian carpet as she left the window and walked restlessly towards the fire. It was beginning to get dark; they couldn't be out much longer. She should appear to have been waiting casually, with no hint of the turmoil she was feeling.

The sudden opening of the door a few minutes later startled her. For all her anticipation of their imminent arrival, she still wasn't quite prepared for the pang she felt when Alex came into the room. Like Ben he had been wearing a thick parka, and although it was unzipped now the soft sheepskin lining framed his lean, attractive face.

And because she had no wish to admire his dark features, or have him examine her own expression too closely, she forced herself to look beyond him for her son. But Alex was on his own; Ben had evidently lingered in the garden, and she rose to her feet automatically, prepared to call him in if necessary.

'He's gone to the bathroom,' Alex remarked flatly before she could detour around him to reach the window. 'He wanted to use the toilet, and I've told him to wash his face and hands. The snow was melting and he's got mud under his fingernails.'

'Oh.'

Sara hoped that her response was sufficiently casual, and glanced behind her at her chair. But the idea of sitting down and allowing Alex to tower over her was not appealing, so she merely moved a little nearer to the fire.

'Are you cold?'

Alex had apparently taken her withdrawal at face value, and despite harbouring an unwilling suspicion that this wasn't the case Sara decided it was easier to do the same. 'Well, you did bring a chill into the room with you,' she offered, attempting a conciliatory tone, and he inclined his head.

'But you don't find the house cold?' he prompted, and she had no difficulty in making a denial.

'It's a lot warmer than Perry Edmunds,' she admitted. 'I'd forgotten how cold England can be. It's a wonder Ben hasn't caught a chill too. He's obviously more resilient than me.'

Alex pushed his hands into his jacket pockets. 'Perhaps it's in his genes,' he remarked quietly. 'All that Viking blood we're supposed to possess. Did you know the Vikings had a settlement not far from here a couple of centuries after the Romans departed? I think they found Northumbria considerably warmer than their predecessors.'

'I expect they did,' said Sara, refusing to be drawn into a discussion of Ben's genes. 'Oh, dear—' she looked towards the windows '—it appears to be raining.'

Alex barely glanced over his shoulder. 'So it does,' he said wryly, and she knew that he wasn't deceived by her obvious change of subject. 'The snow won't last long. It was already thawing.'

'Was it?' Sara wondered how long one small boy could take to use the toilet and wash his face and hands. 'Well, I'm sure Ben's enjoyed himself. He's never seen snow before.'

'No. So he said.' Alex paused, and studied the toe of his leather boot. 'He's a great kid. I like him. Whatever else I might regret, you've made a good job of bringing him up so far.'

'Thanks.' The word almost choked her, but she was not about to lose her temper now. 'His... father...deserves most of the credit, though.' *God*! Why was she stumbling over that word? She licked her lips and continued doggedly, 'Harry had endless patience with Ben.'

'Harry?' Alex's chin lifted until his narrowed eyes were level with hers. 'You're still insisting that Harry was Ben's father?'

'Of course.' Sara wished that her son would come back and put an end to this seemingly interminable interview. 'I—I wish you'd stop pretending you have an ounce of proof to disprove it.' She took a breath. 'If I'm prepared to overlook . . . to overlook what happened and let you be an uncle to Ben, can't you accept that?'

'Not nearly,' retorted Alex harshly, and, stepping closer, he let her feel the heat of his breath on her temple. 'I could break you, do you know that?' he demanded, and although he wasn't touching her Sara could feel every nerve in her body straining to get away from him. His eyes raked her averted face with raw impatience. 'Don't make me do it, Sara. Believe me, you'd regret it.'

Sara felt as if her lungs were burning. 'Threats,' she managed hoarsely. 'Always threats. What do you want me to do, Alex? Hand my son over to you on the strength of your intimidations? Dream on!'

Alex seemed to be considering her words, and although she would have liked to step back from him Sara knew her only salvation lay in convincing him that he didn't—couldn't—scare her.

But just as she was beginning to breathe a little more easily Alex lifted his hand and cupped the vulnerable curve of her neck. And although her withdrawal was automatic his hard fingers allowed no retreat. Exerting what was, for him, only the slightest pressure, his thumb dug into her windpipe so deeply that she knew a bruise would be the least of her worries.

'Oh, Sara,' he said at last, when she gave up the unequal struggle, 'what do I have to do to convince you that in any confrontation between us you're bound to be the loser?'

Sara didn't answer him. She merely pressed her lips together, as if refusing to rise to his deliberate baiting, when in actual fact she didn't trust herself to speak. Alex's thin mouth took on a decidedly mocking slant.

'Tell me,' he said, his thumb moving to stroke the rigid muscles of her jaw, 'didn't Harry ever discuss Ben's conception with you? Didn't he ever wonder why the child was born a bare eight months after you and he were married?'

Sara still maintained her silence, and as if deciding that some other method of persuasion was required Alex brought his other hand up to brush his fingers against her lips. That was harder to ignore. The rough abrasion caused her lips to part, and although she winced at the invasion the pad of one of his fingers touched the soft inner curve of her mouth. At once she could taste the distinctly masculine flavour of him on her tongue, and panic rose helplessly inside her.

'Don't!'

'Don't?' he echoed, and his voice was decidedly husky now. 'Don't touch you—or don't show what a pathetic little liar you are? Come on, Sara; tell me you're not desperate to hide how you really feel.'

'You bastard!'

'That's better.' A curious look of satisfaction crossed his face now. 'I was beginning to think you'd given in without a fight.'

Sara swallowed convulsively. 'You wish.'

'You have no idea what I wish,' he retorted with sudden bitterness. 'But go on—tell me that Harry accepted Ben's appearance without making any comment.'

'He did.'

'And that doesn't strike you as odd?'

'Why should it?' Sara wished desperately that he'd let go of her. Those humiliating fingers were like searing brands against her skin. 'Harry—Harry trusted me.'

'Oh, God!' Alex turned his eyes towards the ceiling for a moment. But although Sara hoped that this might indicate a softening in his attitude his stare was just as cold and contemptuous when it returned to hers. 'Well, we both know how undeserved that was, don't we? Face it, Sara; Harry didn't ask about Ben's conception because he didn't want to hear the answer.'

'No!'

'Yes.' Alex's savage stare was debilitating. 'For heaven's sake, he wasn't a fool. Why do you think he didn't question the fact that you got pregnant so quickly?'

Sara held up her head. 'We had lived together for almost a year before the wedding,' she declared stiffly, hoping that she sounded more convincing than she felt, and Alex uttered a scornful snort.

'But not for six weeks before the actual ceremony,' he reminded her. 'Harry was in Kuwait until two days before the wedding.'

Sara's face flamed. 'It's nothing to do with you—'

'It's everything to do with me,' retorted Alex harshly. 'Why haven't you had any other children? Have you ever asked yourself that?'

'I won't listen to any more of this.'

Sara's nerve gave out, and despite the futility of her efforts earlier she attempted to get free. With shallow breaths, and hands that fumbled wildly to displace those strangely possessive fingers, she pushed against him, unhappily aware as she did so of the overwhelming weakness he inspired.

But on this occasion Alex's tactics changed. Instead of resisting her he let her go, and because she had been prepared to fight she lost her balance, falling against him helplessly—against the fine black silk of his shirt.

The silk was warm from his body—incredibly warm, considering the cold day outside. And sensuous . . . *God*, she thought, nothing had ever felt so sensuous, yet so hard, so masculine, so taut with ridged muscle.

The forbidden thought that Harry's body had never felt so hard was stifled almost before it was born. Harry had never been like Alex; she knew that. God help her, it was why she had gone through with the marriage. Why had she buried her head in the sand, when all her instincts had warned her to tell him what had happened?

She was scrambling away from Alex in a panic when she realised that the hands that had automatically gripped her shoulders to save her were not torturing her any more. And when she darted a glance up at him she found a curious look of disbelief on his face. If she hadn't known better she'd have said his expression was almost desperate, though she still didn't trust the heavy-lidded menace in his eyes.

'Sara...' he said, his voice harsh with feeling, and she wondered for one incredulous moment if she had won. But before she could congratulate herself on her victory he pulled her closer and buried his burning face in her neck.

Horror displaced triumph; disgust overcame fear. Even though her head was still swimming with the realisation that Alex was not as indifferent to her as he'd like her to believe, somehow she found the strength to push him away. Maybe his emotions had blinded him to her reactions, or perhaps the soft pull of her body had momentarily sapped his will. Whatever, Sara found no problem at all in putting the width of the room between them, though her legs were like jelly and she almost fell.

It was just as well that she acted as she did. She had barely reached the comparative safety of the window-seat before her son came into the room with his usual lack of decorum. Skidding to a halt on the carpet, he looked in dismay towards his mother, but although Sara stiffened anxiously his words were as innocent as his face.

'It's raining,' he groaned. 'Oh—blow!'

Sara wondered if she'd ever breathe normally again, but it was almost a relief to answer him. 'Never mind,' she said, wishing that she knew what Alex was thinking at this moment. 'I expect it will snow again. You'll have plenty of other times to enjoy it.'

'Will I?'

Ben addressed his question to his uncle, and under cover of Alex's reply Sara cast a surreptitious glance in his direction. To her relief her brother-in-law seemed to have recovered from whatever madness had gripped him, and had it not been for her own trembling awareness of what had happened she might have believed she'd imagined it.

But she hadn't. For five, maybe ten seconds she had felt the unmistakable pressure of his swollen manhood against her lower body; her stomach still bore the imprint, she was sure; her roiling senses continued to fight the nausea that had gripped her.

Her eyes flickered guiltily down his body as he spoke to Ben, but like any emotions that she had inadvertently stirred his arousal had subsided. His muscled thighs still flexed powerfully beneath the taut cloth of his dark trousers as he bent to pick Ben up, but his mind was in control, as she found when her eyes returned to his face.

'Shall we go?' he asked, intercepting her fleeting appraisal, and she gave a jerky nod of her head.

'But we will come again, won't we?' said Ben, his arms around his uncle's neck. 'I like it here better than at Grandmama's house. It's not so cold and dark.'

'Grandmama's house isn't cold and dark,' said Sara automatically, though even as she said the words she knew they weren't true. But there was no way she was going to allow Ben to dictate their whereabouts, particularly when the alternative was so intolerable.

'Of course you can come again,' Alex declared now, putting Ben on the floor again. 'I want you to come as often as you like.' His eyes were dark and enigmatic as he included Sara in the invitation. 'I'd like you to think of Ragdale as your home. It's what…your father would have wanted.'

CHAPTER NINE

THE journey back to Edmundsfield seemed to take far longer than the journey out had done. Although the two houses were only a few miles apart, the road was narrow and twisting, and Sara felt as if she bore every inch of the way in her bones. If it hadn't been for the fact that Ben kept up an excited monologue for most of the fifteen minutes that it took to reach Perry Edmunds, she knew the silence between her and Alex would have been quite unbearable. As it was, they each appeared to be listening to Ben, though she suspected that, like herself, Alex couldn't have told anyone what the boy said.

To her relief the Reeds had visitors. The sight of the strange car in the drive gave her leave to think that she could make her escape when they got indoors, and the idea of having some time alone before supper seemed briefly more important than protecting her son from Alex.

But although Alex didn't say anything he must have identified the car, and his 'Come and say hello to James and Linda' aborted her careful plans.

'Oh, I don't think . . .' she began stiffly, no more eager to see Linda Erskine than Linda would be to see her, she was sure, but Alex's hand at her elbow was forceful, and once again she was obliged to give in.

And, although she could hardly regard James Erskine as a friend, she was disappointed to find only his wife sitting with Alex's mother, taking tea. Robert too was absent, so she didn't even have his friendly face as support.

112

'So there you are!' exclaimed Elizabeth Reed half-impatiently. 'I was beginning to wonder if something was wrong. I expected you back an hour ago, Alex. Did you go into Corbridge for tea?'

'No.' Alex had released Sara's elbow as soon as he had achieved his objective, and she pressed her arm protectively across her body. 'Ben and I have been having a snow fight—'

'And playing with the sledge,' put in Ben impulsively.

'And Sara's been renewing her acquaintance with the house,' went on his uncle imperviously. 'There have been quite a lot of changes since she was there before.'

Sara could feel the hot colour flooding into her throat, and although she had been about to take her overcoat off now she pretended that her intention had been to draw the collar closer beneath her chin. As it was, her face was probably rosy, but that might be blamed on the fire, though she guessed from Linda's expression that she wasn't deceived.

'How cosy,' she remarked, with a faintly malicious edge to her voice. 'You must be a glutton for punishment, my dear. I can think of nothing more boring than looking round a house some other woman has furnished. Particularly when you know you can't have an opinion.'

Sara hoped her expression didn't show how shocked she suddenly felt. Another woman? she thought painfully. What other woman? If Alex had been married, surely Harry would have told her?

It was more galling for her to realise that it mattered. Despite her dislike—*hatred*?—of her brother-in-law, she found she resented the thought that Harry had kept her in the dark. Yet wasn't that what he might have done, in the circumstances? He had sensed her antagonism towards Alex from the start.

Yet she hadn't been antagonistic towards Alex in the very beginning, she remembered unwillingly. In fact, when Harry had introduced them she'd thought that his brother was a very attractive man. Of course, anyone would have, she defended herself. He had had a glamorous profession. And, on top of that, he'd seemed totally lacking in conceit.

She'd only known Harry for a couple of weeks at that time, and their relationship had scarcely been an intimate one. Having been introduced to him at a party given by her boss, she'd only met him on two other occasions, and, looking back, she had to admit that Harry hadn't seemed too thrilled that his brother should have chosen to come home on the very night he had invited Sara to dinner at the apartment they shared. But Alex's assignments had been unpredictable, to say the least, and he couldn't have known that Harry had organised a rather special evening.

In any event, although Alex had offered to take himself off again, Harry wouldn't hear of it, and the meal had been stretched to feed the three of them. And, if she was honest, Sara knew that she would have to admit that she had enjoyed the evening tremendously. In fact, she remembered, she and Alex had found that they had a lot in common, not least their sense of humour. Her strongest recollection of the evening was one of laughter and relaxation.

Indeed, she had enjoyed herself so much that for several days afterwards she'd known a guilty sense of anticipation every time the phone had rung. She'd told herself that she didn't actually expect Alex to ring her, but the fact remained that she had entertained a fleeting hope that he might.

Of course, he hadn't. Apart from the fact that he'd only seen her as Harry's girlfriend, men like him did not become involved with rather ordinary-looking secretaries. And as if to endorse this belief Harry had let it slip that a famous model's name was currently being linked with that of his brother.

She'd said something rather malicious about that, she remembered broodingly, and afterwards Harry had avoided talking about his brother at all.

And that had seemed to be that.

Alex had departed soon afterwards on yet another overseas posting, and Sara's affair with Harry had deepened into a lasting relationship. By the time Alex had returned to London some three months later she and Harry were discussing living together, and in the excitement of moving to the luxurious three-bedroomed apartment that Harry had found for them she hadn't had time to think about anyone else. Had she...?

'Linda means she gave me some advice when I was choosing the carpets and curtains,' Alex was saying now, and Sara realised that he was trying to ameliorate the other woman's words. 'What are you trying to do?' he added, with just sufficient tolerance in his voice to avoid offending her. 'D'you want Sara to think I've been keeping a woman at Ragdale all these months?'

'I doubt if Sara cares what you've been doing at Ragdale, darling,' Linda countered carelessly. 'And you're not telling me that Karen Summers didn't have some influence on your choice of colours. With hair of that particular shade of red—'

'I really don't think who Alex entertains at Ragdale is the concern of anyone but himself,' inserted his mother rather irritably, and although Sara knew that she should feel grateful for Elizabeth's intervention she couldn't help wondering what the American actress had been doing in Northumberland. Just another example of Alex's rather obvious attraction for women, she thought bitterly. It would be foolish to think that because he hadn't married he'd lived the life of a celibate.

'We saw a fox,' Ben volunteered suddenly, evidently deciding that he had been ignored for far too long. 'Uncle Alex says you're more likely to see them in winter. Its coat looked ever so pretty against the snow.'

'They're vermin,' declared Linda at once with feeling, and when Ben frowned and turned to his mother Sara found her eyes going instinctively to Alex.

'What's vermin?' Ben asked, puzzled yet instinctively knowing that it wasn't a good thing, and his uncle gave Linda another warning stare.

'What Mrs Erskine means is that they're not popular with farmers,' he told the boy gently. 'They're inclined to raid the hen-house, and put the hens off laying lots of lovely eggs.'

'At the least,' remarked Linda, unrepentant. 'They actually kill the chickens, Ben. And lambs, too, if their mother can't defend them.' Her lips twisted, and she met Sara's eyes with pure malice. 'If you want to be a country boy, you have to learn that not everything that looks pretty is pretty.'

'Isn't that the truth?' said Alex harshly, but Ben's response was far less under control.

'What does she mean?' he asked his mother, his jaw quivering unsteadily. 'Does she mean the farmers shoot foxes like those men shot Daddy?'

Sara's stomach hollowed. 'I—' Her eyes sought Alex's again almost disbelievingly, and then she crouched down in front of her son. 'Who—who told you that?' she asked unevenly. 'Who told you that—that some men killed Daddy? Come on, Ben. I want to know. Why haven't you mentioned this before?'

'Is it true?'

There were tears glistening in his eyes now, and Sara wanted nothing so much as to gather him into her arms. But the belief that someone in this house had deliberately frightened the boy with such a story kept her vigilant. It could only have been one of two people: either Mrs Reed or Alex.

'Who told you?' she coaxed, aware that a pregnant silence had fallen around them. Evidently they all wanted to hear his answer, and Sara guessed that at least one of them was feeling the strain.

'I want to go to the toilet,' said Ben, sniffing, and Sara was sure that she heard an audible sigh of relief. But although she cast a look over her shoulder she had no idea who had made the sound.

'Who told you?' she repeated, aware that this probably wasn't the wisest—or the kindest—thing to do but needing to know the truth for her own purposes. For God's sake, she wouldn't have believed that anyone could be so unfeeling. Surely Alex couldn't have done this because she refused to acknowledge his claim?

'I want to use the toilet!' exclaimed Ben with more urgency. 'I really do. I want to—'

'I don't really think we need to hear what you want to do, Ben,' declared his grandmother hurriedly. 'For goodness' sake, Sara, let the child go. We don't want him having an accident in here, do we?'

'But—'

'I think my mother's right,' said Alex from behind her. He gestured to the little boy. 'Run along, Ben. And don't forget to wash your hands afterwards.'

Ben didn't need any further encouragement. He darted round his mother and out of the room without a backward glance, and Sara was left to get to her feet, feeling as if she had been reprimanded instead.

But if Ben was happy to obey his uncle's commands she certainly was not, and when she turned on Alex her eyes were bright with anger. 'How dare you?' she exclaimed, relieved to find that her voice didn't betray the tremor that was making itself felt throughout the rest of her body. 'When I want your advice I'll ask for it. And that includes telling Ben how his father died!'

Sara did not join her in-laws for supper. She sent a message via Mrs Fraser that she had a headache, which was nothing less than the truth, though the reason for its presence was rather different from any she'd have cared to admit.

Time—and a certain belated sense of remorse—had altered her interpretation of the events of the afternoon, and although she still viewed what had happened between herself and Alex at Ragdale with disgust she couldn't deny that she'd been too quick to cast him in the role of informer. After all, she had no proof that it had been Alex who'd discussed Harry's death with the boy, and by the time he'd come out of the bathroom Ben himself had conveniently forgotten who it was who'd related the story.

Of course, Sara had been tempted to press him further, but because she didn't really know how much—or even if—he understood the topic had had to be abandoned. The last thing she wanted was to frighten him again, even if it meant that her own feelings of frustration had inevitably hardened into a gnawing ache in her temples.

She eventually decided to have an early night and seek the oblivion that could only be found in sleep. But once again she found that her efforts were thwarted. She couldn't sleep; she couldn't even relax; her mind was buzzing with the events of the day and nothing she did seemed to stop it.

It was useless telling herself that once New Year was over she could put Ragdale, Perry Edmunds and even Edmundsfield itself behind her. The days until that could be accomplished seemed very long indeed.

She realised that going to Alex's house had been her biggest mistake so far. Like an old wound that in the right circumstances might still prove vulnerable, the memories that visit had evoked now lay before her like an open sore. She hadn't really destroyed all those memories, she fretted. She'd simply covered them with a veneer.

It was a veneer that Alex's behaviour this afternoon had torn aside, she acknowledged bitterly. Until he'd touched her she'd almost believed that she could come away unscathed. But his hands on her arms, on her body had shredded her control. She could still feel his arousal against her belly.

God!

She rolled desperately onto her stomach, trying to still its queasy churning. She felt hot; she felt sick; every inch of her skin felt clammy. If she'd still been living in Brazil, she'd have been half-afraid that she was sickening for some tropical disease.

But, of course, she wasn't, although the feelings that Alex had resurrected were not unlike a disease in themselves. From the very beginning he'd had that effect on her. And, although she'd fought the temptation, ultimately she'd succumbed...

Looking back, she knew that she should never have let Harry persuade her to spend those final few weeks before the wedding at Perry Edmunds. Just because he had had to leave for Kuwait rather earlier than they had anticipated, he'd suggested that Sara should spend the time getting to know his parents. He'd feel happier, he'd said, knowing that she wasn't in London on her own. And although she'd protested that she'd lived on her own for several years before they'd got together he'd asked her to do it, just for him.

It had been one of those 'if' situations, Sara thought ruefully now—if she hadn't given in her notice when he'd suggested, if she hadn't admitted that she'd be lonely while he was away, if she'd insisted that she had plenty to occupy her, instead of letting him arrange it before he went.

Of course, Harry hadn't known that Alex was staying at Perry Edmunds any more than she had. The last card they had had from him had been from some unpronounceable village near Sarajevo, and had he not suffered a minor wound from flying shrapnel her visit would have passed without event. Another if, she thought unhappily. Though when she'd first arrived she'd been grateful that he was there.

She'd been aware that Elizabeth Reed didn't think that she was good enough for her son ever since their first brief visit to Perry Edmunds. It had been just after they'd moved in together, and after spending a weekend skiing in Scotland they'd called in on Harry's parents on their way back to London.

And it had been obvious after just an hour in Mrs Reed's company that she had had someone else in mind for him. That Harry had found the idea amusing hadn't made Sara feel any better. But then, she recalled, he had always been inclined to bury his head in the sand.

In any event, she'd been forced to view her visit on this occasion with rather more enthusiasm. She had been offered an invitation, after all, and she was now wearing Harry's ring. And six weeks wasn't so long, she'd consoled herself firmly. She might even get to feel at home at last.

Her first intimation of impending disaster had come when she'd found Alex waiting for her at Newcastle airport. But although she'd been vaguely alarmed to see him he'd treated her in such an unthreatening fashion that she'd relaxed and told herself that she was glad she wouldn't have to face Harry's parents on her own.

And after a few days she'd been inordinately glad of his company. She wasn't used to country living in any form, and that first week at Perry Edmunds had been bleak. Despite the fact that it was early summer, the weather had been appalling. When it wasn't raining there was an icy wind blowing across the moors, and she'd huddled over the fire most of the time. She didn't ride, she didn't play golf—she couldn't share in any of her prospective in-laws' interests. And what with Robert's work for local government and Elizabeth's support of the Women's Institute they were seldom at home.

Looking back, Sara had to admit that perhaps she hadn't tried hard enough to fit in. If she'd taken riding lessons, for example, or insisted on joining the golf club where Mrs Reed played... But the truth was that Harry's father had always seemed too busy to accommodate her, and Elizabeth Reed had actively discouraged any participation in her affairs.

'I'm sure you'd be bored to tears,' she'd declared one morning when Sara had suggested that she might join her and Linda on the course. She'd slapped her gloves against her thigh and smiled maliciously. 'Why don't you ask Alex to take you into Newcastle? You can shop there to your heart's content.'

The implied criticism had been obvious, and Sara hadn't made the mistake of asking again. Harry must have been mad to suggest that she come here, she'd thought unhappily. She'd wished that she could just pack up and go home.

But because she'd had no desire to appear intimidated, and because she'd longed to wipe the smirk off Mrs Reed's face, she'd said carelessly, 'Perhaps I will. Where is Alex, by the way? I haven't seen him this morning. He may not want to take me. He is on sick leave, isn't he?'

'Oh, I'm sure Alex would be happy to make an exception where you're concerned,' returned Mrs Reed smoothly, with none of the censure that Sara had half expected. 'And I think he's down at the stables. You

might try there, at least. He often helps Darcy to clean
out the stalls.'

'Thanks.'

As Elizabeth Reed sauntered out of the room, an elegant figure in her checked trousers and cashmere
sweater, Sara got reluctantly to her feet. Despite her
bravado, the idea of approaching Alex for a favour
wasn't appealing. She was only his brother's fiancée.
Why should he care about her?

In the event, Alex himself appeared as she was sum-
moning the courage to go and find him. 'Going out?'
he asked, noticing the warm navy jacket that she had
put on over her shirt and jeans, and Sara felt her cheeks
turn pink.

'Sort of,' she admitted. 'I was coming to look for you,
actually. Your mother said you were down at the stables,
and I—I wondered if you wanted—' she baulked at the
idea of asking him to take her out '—um—company.'

Alex's lean face took on a wry expression. 'You wanted
my company?' he queried, his tone one of disbelief. 'I
thought you didn't like me. You looked positively horrified when I met you at the airport.'

'I didn't.'

'You did.' Alex regarded her with some amusement.
'Didn't Harry warn you I was staying here?'

As Sara didn't believe for a minute that Harry had
known his brother was home, it was easier to avoid that
question, and, pushing her hands into her jacket pockets,
she affected a rueful smile. 'It looks like there's been a
misunderstanding,' she said. 'I can't imagine why you
would think I don't like you. You're Harry's brother—
my prospective brother-in-law. I hope we can be friends.'

Alex's mouth twisted. 'Do you?' he said rather enig-
matically. And then he went on, 'OK. So do I. How
about toasting our conciliation over lunch? There's a

little pub just outside Hexham that serves a really decent steak.'

'All right.'

Sara found that she liked the idea of having lunch with him far more than asking him to take her to Newcastle. Whatever Elizabeth Reed thought, she didn't enjoy spending all her time shopping, and the prospect of seeing more of the area was one which she wholly embraced.

And, just as she'd thought on that unforgettable occasion when he'd joined her and Harry for the evening, Alex was fun to be with. He was much less serious-minded than his brother, and although he accepted its precepts he enjoyed making fun of the Establishment. He had a host of anecdotes about people whom Sara had hitherto only heard of through the media, and it was reassuring to discover that everyone had their faults and that even golden idols sometimes had feet of clay.

She couldn't remember ever laughing so much, and it wasn't until she met Alex's eyes and saw the lazy warmth reflected in their depths that she was unexpectedly silenced. There was such a wealth of sensuality in his gaze, and an attraction which she uneasily recognised as being mutual. Without her really being aware of it he'd got under her skin, and she sensed even then that she was in danger of doing something really stupid.

'Don't stop,' he urged her gently when she put a nervous hand across her mouth. 'You've got the most infectious laugh I've ever heard. It's delightful.'

But the spell she had been under was broken. Reality was reasserting itself, and with it the awareness that her first instincts about Alex had been correct. He was dangerous—and she'd be a fool if she forgot it. It was Harry she cared about, Harry she loved, and he deserved so much better than this.

Somehow she managed to get through the rest of the day without making any more mistakes—a circumstance which persuaded her that there was no reason why she shouldn't accept another invitation from him when it was offered.

After all, she assured herself, she couldn't be expected to spend the next few weeks twiddling her thumbs, and she owed it to herself—and to Harry—to prove that she could associate with Alex without becoming infatuated with him. So long as she remembered not to take him seriously she'd be OK. And with Harry's ring on her finger she felt that she had a fail-safe talisman against any male sorcery.

She was surprised at Elizabeth Reed's reaction to their friendship. She had expected Harry's mother to look rather disapprovingly on her association with her younger son, but for some reason the other woman seemed to regard their relationship with a benign satisfaction, as if she herself were responsible for its initiation.

Whatever, in the days that followed Alex devoted much of his time to familiarising Sara with the surrounding area, even taking her as far as the borders of Scotland and across to Lindisfarne, the holy island, separated from the mainland by a causeway that was flooded at high tide.

The weather, too, relented, and they were treated to long days of warmth and sunshine when it was almost impossible to believe that only days before the temperature had hovered just a few degrees above zero. Sara took to wearing short-sleeved shirts and shorts for touring, and her normally pale skin acquired a faint tan.

Of course, to begin with she didn't expect it to last. She awakened every morning anticipating that today would be the day when Alex would tell her that he was leaving, but it didn't happen. And when she eventually got around to questioning him about his future plans he admitted that he should have returned to London days ago. But for reasons which she chose not to pursue he told his employers that his injuries weren't healing as quickly as he'd expected, and that his doctor had recommended several more weeks of rest and recuperation.

Sara knew that this wasn't true. Not so far as his physical injuries were concerned, at any rate. She'd seen the scars that bisected his thigh during the first week of her visit. She'd been collecting a paperback that she was reading from her room when he'd emerged from his mother's bedroom carrying a tube of what Sara assumed was antiseptic cream.

Thankfully, he hadn't seen her. The fact that he had been wearing a pair of boxer shorts and nothing else would have embarrassed both of them, and she'd quickly slipped back into her room until he'd gone—but not before she'd seen the peppering of grapeshot that marked his brown flesh—or the disturbing mound of his sex, outlined so clearly beneath the soft fabric of his shorts.

About three weeks before Sara was due to return to London Alex asked if she'd like to go to a party. It was being held at the Adams' house in honour of Linda's twenty-fifth birthday. He'd been invited, he said, and naturally he'd asked if he could bring her along.

Sara wasn't keen. The brushes she had had with Linda so far had not encouraged her to think of the other girl as a friend, and the idea of going to her house, of laying herself open to the kind of criticism that only Elizabeth Reed and Linda could deliver was not appealing. She was already aware that Linda regarded her as a rival—which was ludicrous—and turning up as Alex's 'date' could only exacerbate the situation.

But when, in a moment of weakness, she confided her fears to Alex he assured her that she was imagining things. No matter what she might have been told, he and

Linda had never been more than casual friends. They'd known one another for a long time, it was true, but there had never been any question of a romance between them, and if anyone chose to think differently it was hardly his fault.

Besides, he added drily, if people had been going to talk about *their* relationship, they'd had ample opportunity during the past couple of weeks, when he'd been escorting her all over the county. Surely if they had been going to commit some terrible indiscretion they'd have already done it, not waited for such a public occasion to advertise their guilt?

Of course, she had to admit that he was right. No woman in her right mind would go to a party with a man whom she was supposedly having a clandestine affair with. It would look far more suspicious if she refused the invitation. And, after all, in less than a month she was getting married...

CHAPTER TEN

ABANDONING any hope of getting any rest, Sara got up now and padded over to the window. The cold night air plucked at the thin folds of her nightgown as she perched on the window-seat, but for once she hardly felt it. Her skin was still hot, feverish even, but she couldn't help it. The memories she'd spent the last five years suppressing just kept on coming in a never-ending stream...

The day before Linda's birthday Alex took Sara to see a house that was for sale in Ragdale. The house was unoccupied, its elderly owners having moved to warmer climes, but it was still fully furnished in a style that must have been popular in the twenties.

The house was known, rather grandly, as Ragdale Hall. It was the biggest house in a village that boasted only a handful of farms and their accompanying cottages, and was badly in need of refurbishment and repair. The extensive gardens were a jungle of overgrown shrubs and creepers, and there were weeds sprouting all over the drive. But the potential for improvement was there, and Sara could quite see why someone would bother with it. The view from the windows across the windswept countryside was quite beautiful.

'What do you think?' asked Alex after she'd seen the sitting room and the dining room and examined the ancient fixtures in the kitchen. The windows were dirty, of course, and the dust lay thick on most of the old cabinets, but there wasn't any dampness that she could see.

'I think it needs a small fortune spending on it,' she declared at last, running a rueful finger over the chipped white sink. 'But as a house I like it. The rooms are light and spacious. It's got plenty of room to expand. And although I don't know much about these things it seems quite... solid.'

'It is.' Alex glanced about him with a certain pride of ownership. 'I've already had my father check it out for cracks or leaks. He says it needs a damp course, and central heating, naturally. But other than that there's little structurally wrong with it.'

Sara stared at him. 'You've bought it?' she exclaimed disbelievingly.

'Not yet.' Alex shook his head. 'But I'm thinking about it. It's not often houses like this come on the market in this area. And I rather fancy having a proper home of my own.'

'But you've got the apartment,' she ventured.

'In London—I know.' He shrugged. 'But an apartment's not the same as owning a house. For one thing—' he hesitated '—you can't bring up a family in an apartment. Children need a garden. Don't you agree?'

'I—' Sara was nonplussed. For some ridiculous reason she had never thought of Alex getting married and having children. Somehow he'd always seemed so independent, so unshackled, so unwilling to be tied down. The idea of him as a husband and father was curiously unacceptable.

And because she was afraid that whatever answer she gave would sound like griping she avoided saying anything by sauntering out into the hall. The stained-glass window that glinted at the curve of the stairs gave her an excuse to change the subject. Gesturing towards it, she made some inane remark about its vivid colours, and Alex suggested that she should take a closer look.

It wasn't exactly what she had been aiming for, but anything was better than discussing his personal plans for the future, and after admiring the fluted panes that had been shaped to form a kind of fan it was only natural that she should follow him upstairs.

There were five bedrooms and a boxroom, which Alex said might convert to a bathroom if he did decide to buy. The main bathroom, like the kitchen downstairs, seemed to have been installed when the house was built, with the lavatory taking pride of place on a raised platform.

'I guess that's why people used to call it the throne,' remarked Alex humorously, and for all her nervousness Sara had to laugh.

'Well, it was an exciting innovation,' she teased. 'I bet when this house was built it was quite a novelty. In those days people bathed in tubs in front of the fire, and used a little shed at the bottom of the garden.'

'Did you?' asked Alex mischievously, and Sara waved a mocking fist in front of his face.

'I'm not that old,' she retorted. Then, tossing her head mock-haughtily, she added, 'I wasn't speaking from experience. Some of us have read about these things at school.'

'School!' said Alex in mock admiration. 'The lady's got an education. Now, why didn't I think of that before?'

'Perhaps because *you* haven't?' suggested Sara cheekily, and then, half-afraid of the glint of recklessness in his eyes, she made a strategic retreat onto the landing. 'Um . . .' She strove urgently for some other innocuous comment to make, and when nothing was forthcoming pushed open a door they'd hitherto not observed. 'What's in here?'

'A sewing room, I think.'

Alex was right behind her, his hand reaching past her to propel the door wider. His breath was warm on her neck, where the loose neckline of her man's shirt was inclined to slip off one shoulder.

The heat of his body seemed to surround her; his distinctively male scent, which mingled the flavours of pine and sandalwood with the humid smell of his sweat, invaded her nostrils. She'd never been so conscious of any man as she was of him at that moment, and her strongest impulse was to give in to her needs and lean back against him.

Of course, she didn't. Even though the hot awareness of what he was doing to her drenched her senses, she forced herself to stare into the sun-filled room. Dust motes rose in the draught from the opening of the door, but the images that Sara was seeing were all inside her head.

His dark face taunted her from every dazzling corner of the tiny apartment—that humorous dark face, whose lazy eyes and sensual mouth aroused such sinful needs inside her. She could feel the sinuous power of him, remember how he'd looked that morning weeks ago when she'd seen him coming out of his mother's bedroom. Even his hand, splayed against the door, invited her to feel those long, narrow fingers against her flesh.

Her breathing had quickened, and she started violently when Alex spoke in her ear. 'You know, the past had its advantages. I rather like the idea of bathing before the fire. In those days this was probably the maid's room. D'you think she'd have been willing to scrub her master's back?'

Sara swallowed, struggling to regain her lost composure. 'In—in the bathroom?' she stammered. 'Oh— I think her—her mistress would have had something to say about that.'

'Not if she didn't know,' pointed out Alex gently, tugging the slipping shirt back onto her shoulder. 'I think there's something rather exciting about doing something that's forbidden. The sweetest fruit is always out of reach.'

Sara licked her lips. 'Is it?'

'Eve thought so,' he intoned softly, and Sara knew that she couldn't stand this game of verbal cat-and-mouse any longer.

'Look what happened to her!' she exclaimed, swinging round to face him. 'Poor Adam had to share her awful fate.'

'Perhaps he didn't mind,' said Alex thoughtfully, making no effort to step aside, and Sara realised that she'd made a serious mistake. By turning to face him she'd only revealed her anxiety to him, and she wished she'd had the sense to move away.

'Does it matter?' she asked tersely, concentrating on the dark curl of fine hair that poked out of the opened collar of his shirt. 'Oughtn't we to be going?' She glanced ostentatiously at her watch. 'It's nearly half past twelve. We'll be late for lunch.'

Alex's humour departed. 'Are you hungry?' he asked, and she was aware of his eyes moving searchingly over her. He forced a smile—at least, she thought it was forced; there was little warmth in it—and made a rueful sound. 'I'm not much of a host, am I?'

How was she supposed to answer that?

Realising that she was in danger of making this situation even worse, Sara compelled herself to look up into his face. 'As it isn't your house it doesn't apply,' she said tightly, striving for sanity. 'But... thank you for showing it to me. If—if you do decide to buy, I hope you'll be very happy—'

'Do you?' He didn't let her finish, and before she could apprehend what he might mean by it his hands ran possessively up her arms. 'Do you really?' he added, his thumbs rubbing the cloth on her shoulders. 'Don't you really care who I live with here?'

Sara's breathing felt stifled, and because her mind was already spinning with the thoughts she had had earlier it wasn't easy to find an impersonal response. 'I—I— why should I?' she fumbled, wishing that she could manage a condescending smile. 'Um—I'm sure whoever you—um—decide to marry Harry and I will—'

'I'm not talking about Harry,' said Alex steadily, his fingers invading the neckline of her shirt. His eyes dropped to follow their progress, his voice becoming soft with wonder. 'Did anyone ever tell you you have really beautiful skin?'

Sensitive skin certainly, thought Sara, dry-mouthed, knowing that she should push his hands away. But that sinful feeling she had had earlier was returning to torment her, making her curious to know how far he was prepared to let this go.

And then he kissed her.

She hadn't expected him to—at least, that was what she told herself as his lips brushed sensually over hers. That was why she wasn't prepared for it, why her jaw sagged and his probing tongue had easy access to her mouth. It wasn't a violent kiss. He didn't need to coax her, or force her, or use any of his undoubted wealth of experience to make her do anything she didn't want to do. He simply held her and took possession. And there wasn't a damn thing she could do about it.

Initially she tried not to respond, not to give him the satisfaction of knowing how helpless she felt, but his hands, cupping her neck, defeated her. The feel of his thumbs massaging her skin, tracing the slender column of her throat, was mindlessly sensual, the warmth rising from the turned-back sleeves of his shirt filling her lungs with the scent of his heated flesh.

Oh, God...

She lifted her hands then to push him away, but instead of pounding against his chest they refused to do her bidding. Her fingers spread and then clenched tight about his wrists, reducing her world to the sight and sound and feel of only him. She could feel his bones, taut within their narrow casing of muscle and sinew, sense the latent strength he was holding back from her. With every fibre of her being she longed to press herself against him, and her strength to resist this madness was slipping away.

And then, when all seemed lost, Alex seemed to come to his senses. Before she could condemn herself completely by giving in to her treacherous feelings, Alex uttered a muffled oath and pulled away. As she swayed dizzily, struggling to regain her senses, he braced himself with one hand against the door.

'I'm sorry,' he said harshly, raking agitated fingers through his hair, gripping the back of his neck with obvious frustration. 'Is this going to be a problem? Hell— I don't know what to say. I'm a bloody fool, and I'll quite understand if you feel you can't forgive me.'

Sara was endeavouring to get over the appalling fact that she felt as if someone had just kicked her in the stomach. 'I—forget it,' she got out unsteadily, realising what she had to do. 'It wasn't important,' she added, lifting her shoulders in a careless gesture of dismissal. 'I guess we—both—just got carried away.'

It was the right way to handle it, she knew that as soon as she saw the way his eyes darkened at her apparent indifference. Nevertheless, she needed to put some space between them without delay. Swinging about, she took stock of her bearings, and then advanced purposefully into the room.

She didn't have a lot of choice with him blocking the only exit, she thought tensely. And, feigning a casual interest in her surroundings, she struggled to get her breathing back on track. But her heart was racing wildly, its beat ringing in her ears, thudding against her skull like a thing possessed.

There was an old chaise longue beneath the round, old-fashioned window, and she dropped one knee upon it and pretended to study the view. But all she was conscious of was a kind of reckless elation, and the sensual taste of Alex on her tongue...

'Are you sure you're OK?'

Oh, God, he was behind her!

While she had been striving to attain some measure of sanity, Alex had followed her across the room, and now his hand on her shoulder was urging her to turn around. But how could she look at him when she couldn't control her senses? How could she let him look into her eyes when she was afraid of what he might see? How could she keep her head when the blood was like liquid fire in her veins?

'I'm fine,' she said hurriedly, hoping that he would take the hint and leave her. All she needed was a few minutes alone and she'd be all right. Turning Harry's ring, she pressed the square-cut sapphire into her finger. But even the pain that she was inflicting on herself wasn't enough.

'Sara...'

Dear Lord, even her name on his lips sounded soft and sensual. She could imagine how it would sound spoken against her skin. His hand lifted and, thinking she was safe, she glanced up at him—only to find that she wasn't safe at all.

He was still there, looking down at her, and the knee that she had been resting on suddenly buckled beneath her. With a little sound she subsided onto her bottom, and as if she had offered him an invitation to join her Alex lowered his weight beside her.

Even then she thought she might be imagining the tension. After all, he had only kissed her before breaking away. And although he was lounging beside her he wasn't touching her. His arms were outspread at either side of him in an attitude that was more indolent than threatening.

She bent her head to examine a speck of dust on her jeans, unknowingly exposing the vulnerable curve of her nape to his gaze. Her hair—a silky, bronze-coloured bob—slid aside, screening his face from her, and the first hint she had of his intentions was when his forefinger stroked a sinuous path from her hairline to the tipped collar of her shirt.

'Oh, Sara,' he said, his voice low and defeated. 'Do you have any idea what you're doing to me?'

Sara's reaction was more defensive than anything. 'Me?' She almost squeaked the word, turning to look at him with wide, indignant eyes. 'I don't know—what you—'

But she foundered helplessly before the undisguised hunger in his face, and when he cupped her neck with his hand and brought her towards him she didn't resist.

'Madness,' he breathed harshly, but that didn't stop his mouth from finding hers with fierce possession, didn't stop his hands from sliding down her back and settling heavily on the slender curve of her hips. 'Summer madness,' he added against her lips, his tongue running wetly along the seam. 'Open your mouth for me, Sara. At least let me put my tongue inside you.'

Sara's senses swam. Her lips parted almost without her volition, and his tongue thrust greedily into her mouth. There was something so mindlessly pleasurable in that urgent possession that any thought she might have had of resisting him was drowned beneath a wave of pure sensation. No one—certainly not Harry—had ever aroused such a powerful surge of need inside her, and her legs splayed helplessly as he bore her back against the faded cushions.

'God, you taste so good,' he groaned, supporting himself above her, and Sara felt the blood rise hotly to the surface of her skin. 'I swore I could handle this but, God, you're driving me insane!'

The knowledge that he must have considered making love to her before should have brought her to her senses, but it didn't. In spite of everything she felt curiously unalarmed, as if what was about to happen was as inevitable as night following day. She'd known that it was going to happen, she thought dizzily, and there wasn't a single thing she could do to stop him.

Alex brought one hand up to slide the neck of her shirt aside, his tongue finding the tiny hollows that marked her collar-bone, dipping into each one and sealing them with his lips. Her shoulder lifted at every sensual caress, and she was unsurprised when the cloth slipped aside, exposing the upper curve of her breast to his sultry gaze.

A button popped beneath his careless fingers, and then another and another, until her shirt was open right down the front. Underneath, the lacy bra she was wearing was little protection from his avid gaze, and with an ease which she could only envy he slipped his hand beneath her back and released the catch.

Her breasts spilled into his waiting hands, and she shivered uncontrollably as he looked down at his bounty. Then his eyes lifted to hers again, and she was suddenly sweating beneath their heat. 'Can I?' he asked huskily, but he didn't require an answer. It wasn't until he bent his head and took one rosy nipple between his teeth that she realised what he'd meant.

A sensation of mingled pain and exquisite pleasure had her reaching convulsively for his head, her fingers winding into his hair, almost dragging it from his scalp.

It wasn't until he bit down rather harder than she had anticipated that she had a notion that she was hurting him, and she caught her lower lip between her teeth as he moved over her again.

'Savage little beast, aren't you?' he breathed unsteadily, but her own needs were tearing at her now, and, gripping the sides of his head, Sara brought his mouth back to hers.

His weight was on her, crushing her against the worn cushions, the rough denim of his shirt rubbing painfully against her tender breasts. Yet it wasn't really painful, she acknowledged confusedly. There was something infinitely enjoyable about the sensation, and while Alex's lips slanted eagerly over hers she shifted sensually beneath him, allowing him to feel her swollen nipples for himself.

Considering the way she had behaved from the distance of years, she had to admit that she had asked for trouble. It was the first—and only—time that she had ever acted in such a way. She wasn't the type to behave provocatively, wantonly; she'd always been in control of her emotions. But with Alex she'd had no inhibitions. She'd sensed that whatever she did he wouldn't turn her away.

The image of how she must have looked to him disturbed her more than she wanted to admit. Had she really lain beneath him, with her shirt unfastened and her bra pushed up above her unfettered breasts? There was something so squalid about the whole scene in her imagination. Yet at the time all she'd felt was an unrestricted pleasure.

And there was no doubt that Alex had enjoyed seeing her that way. The words he'd whispered to her as he'd laid a trail of kisses from the quivering curve of her lips to the creamy fullness of her breasts had left her breathless. No one had ever said such things to her before; no one had ever made her feel as if her body was a temple, and he had been a willing supplicant.

But it hadn't been enough that she had been half-naked. She'd wanted to feel his hard, muscular body against hers. And while her lips had been uttering faint little cries of frustration her fingers had been attempting to peel his shirt from his shoulders. But the buttonholes had seemed too small for her fumbling efforts, and, growing impatient, Alex had pulled away.

Not realising his intentions, Sara remembered that she had gone after him then, tearing off her shirt and bra and winding her bare arms about his neck. 'Don't go,' she'd breathed, pressing her mouth into his neck.

His savage 'I don't intend to' had been smothered by the urgency of her lips.

He'd thrown off his shirt while she'd tantalised him with her tongue, learning the contours of his mouth while he cast the garment away. Then, to her satisfaction, he'd pushed her down onto the couch and covered her whole body with his.

She had been able to feel his arousal, pressing against the junction of her legs, and hadn't been able to resist touching its rigid strength. Even through the taut fabric she had felt it pulsing against her hand, but when her fingers had sought his zip he'd jerked away.

'God—don't,' he said harshly, and then, seeing her hurt expression, he groaned. 'I'm only human, woman,' he told her thickly. 'What in hell are you trying to do to me?'

Sara trembled. 'I thought—'

'I know what you thought,' he interrupted, sliding down her body to trace the outline of her navel with his tongue. 'You thought I'd like it, hmm?' And at her somewhat convulsive nod he made a rueful sound. 'I do,' he said, his voice smothered against the soft skin of her stomach. 'More—much more—than you like this.'

Sara doubted whether that was possible. As the button at her waist parted from its fastening and he pressed his face into the opening exposed by her sliding zip her legs splayed in helpless abandon. Her hands slid down her body in a frenzied imitation of what she wanted him to do with the rest of her clothes and, as if aware of her eagerness, Alex hooked his thumbs into the loops at the waistband of her jeans and eased them over her hips.

That still left the lacy panties that matched the bra she had already discarded, but Alex seemed in no hurry to remove them. On the contrary, he seemed to be getting a distinct pleasure from watching her restless confusion, and when he bent his head and caressed with his tongue an errant, bronze-coloured curl that had escaped from the leg of her panties she almost climaxed. Between her legs a pulse was beating wildly, and she could feel her readiness for him in every slick fold.

With one finger he eased the lace aside and then stroked the damp curls that quivered beneath his hand. Pressing between them, he found the throbbing nub that ached for his touch, and then, finding no resistance, he probed deeper.

'Is that good?' he asked huskily as she arched against him, and when she could only move her head in a gesture of total acquiescence he allowed his tongue to take the place of his finger.

Almost immediately she felt herself losing control. Pleasure swept over her in hot, pulsing waves and there was nothing she could do about it. 'Please—Alex—' she begged, hardly knowing what she was saying in her mindless state, and he uttered a sound of satisfaction as she drenched him with her sweetness.

She was still lamenting her loss of control when Alex moved over her. While she had been drowning in pleasure he had shed the rest of his clothes, and, nudging her legs even wider apart, he came to lie between them. Now she could feel his arousal nudging the damp core of her womanhood, and although she'd been sure that she'd spoiled it for both of them excitement was stirring again in the pit of her stomach.

'I—I—don't know if—' she began unsteadily, and he raised himself on his elbows to look down at the sensual splay of her body.

'What?' he asked, watching her face as he touched her there, where every nerve in her body suddenly seemed to be located. 'What don't you know?'

'I've already—that is—'

'I know.' His mouth took on a sensual curve. 'So what?'

'Well, I don't—I haven't ever—'

'Climaxed more than once?'

She felt her face burn. 'Well—yes.'

'You will.' He pushed himself gently against her. 'I promise.'

And she did, so many times, in fact, that by the time Alex collapsed upon her she was incapable of doing anything but closing her eyes and giving in to the exhaustion that gripped her...

Sara shivered. Why was she remembering that now? she wondered unhappily. She didn't want to think about Alex in that way. She wanted to forget every detail of that sordid encounter.

Only it hadn't seemed sordid at the time, she admitted to herself wearily. And, while she might tell herself that it had just been good sex, in her heart she knew that it had been more than that for her.

From the moment when Alex had started to make love to her she'd known that she would never feel the same again. She hadn't wanted to compare his lovemaking with Harry's, but there had been no doubt that their two bodies had fitted together like halves of a whole. When he'd withdrawn so far from her before thrusting into her again, she'd felt as if she might die of the aching need he was arousing inside her. And when he'd dipped his head to kiss her she'd wrapped her legs about his waist and her arms around his neck.

She remembered how he had drawn back to watch her with all the indulgence of a master, as his body played with hers. With his head thrown back and sweat beading on his forehead, attesting to the control he was exercising to bring her body to its pinnacle of fulfilment, he'd shown a patience that she wouldn't have believed he had. He'd watched her with a heavy-lidded intensity, and she'd watched him, and marvelled at his touch.

But she'd touched him too, she recalled almost unwillingly. Touched him, and caressed him, and run her palms over the hair-roughened skin of his chest. She even remembered the constriction of his muscles as her hand had found the place where they were joined...

Of course, that controlled performance had eventually given way to an urgent possession. But by then time had ceased to mean a thing. She had peaked so many times, each climax greater than the last, and when he'd cupped her bottom in his hands and swept her over the final precipice she'd cried out her pleasure against his shuddering release...

CHAPTER ELEVEN

WHEN Sara had awakened she'd been alone in the little sewing room.

At first she hadn't known where she was. She'd stared blankly at the grey ceiling, trying to make some sense of her surroundings, but it had been the draught of cool air against her naked body that had brought her somewhat dazedly to her senses.

She'd come up off the couch with scant regard for her sore and aching body. Beyond the windows the sun had been well past its meridian, and there had been shadows on the fields that hadn't been there before. She'd dressed hurriedly, as if by covering her nakedness she could cover the awful guilt that had suddenly gripped her. But her clothes hadn't hidden the panic that had flowered inside.

She had just finished fastening her shirt when Alex had appeared in the doorway.

She hadn't known what she had expected from him—shame, anger, embarrassment? Perhaps an amalgam of all three. In fact, his expression had been strangely gentle, and she'd wondered with a bitter pang if he was feeling sorry for her now.

'Hi,' he said, compounding her belief that that was his attitude. 'I was beginning to wonder—are you OK?'

Sara didn't think before answering him. 'Of course,' she said shortly. 'Why shouldn't I be?' And then, because she didn't want to hear the answer to that, she went on, 'It's late.'

'After three o'clock,' he conceded evenly, revealing that it was later than she'd thought. He propped his

142

shoulder against the jamb. 'Are you hungry? I guess we could get a sandwich in Corbridge.'

'I don't want anything,' said Sara hurriedly. 'I just want to go home. Well—back to your parents' house, anyway,' she amended. 'I don't know what they'll think about us being out so long.'

Alex's mouth thinned slightly. 'Does it matter?'

'Does it matter?' Sara was incensed, as much by her own feelings of shame and helplessness as by the way he was acting. 'Of course it matters,' she retorted sharply. 'I've got to explain my absence. I'm not a free spirit like you.'

This last was said with a very definite edge to her voice, and Alex could have been in no doubt as to the way she intended to play it. She closed her mind to any awareness of her own participation in what had happened. So far as she was concerned he had made all the running.

He straightened, and she had to drag her eyes away from the powerful thigh muscles that flexed beneath his jeans. But she was aware of his displeasure. She couldn't help it. Where Alex was concerned she'd lost a layer of skin.

'Does that mean you don't intend to tell Harry what's happened?' he enquired tautly, and Sara found the strength to return his stare.

'Tell Harry?' she exclaimed. 'For heaven's sake, you must be joking! Why would I tell my fiancé that his brother seduced the woman he's going to marry?'

There was no mistaking Alex's anger now. 'You're crazy!'

'I am?' She managed to sound almost amused by the accusation. 'It's you who's crazy if you think I'm going to ruin my life over someone like you.'

'Someone like me?' Alex echoed ominously, but Sara was too wound up to stop.

'Yes,' she said. 'Harry warned me about you in the beginning.' Which wasn't strictly true, but she thought it found its mark. 'He told me what a poseur you were. How you liked your freedom. All the women you've known—in the biblical sense, of course.'

She didn't know if he believed her. She told herself that she didn't care. It was sufficient to know that for once in his life he hadn't had it all his own way. She hated him now as she'd never hated him before.

She said a lot more, most of it eliciting no response from him whatsoever. Indeed, she thought that he was stunned by the vituperation issuing from her tongue. But he let her babble on, expunging all her guilt in accusation. Until she too fell silent, and turned away.

'Shall we go?'

His enquiry was almost impersonal, and Sara's eyes, lingering on the chaise longue a moment longer than was acceptable, abruptly closed. 'Of course,' she said, swinging about and approaching him. 'We'll tell your parents we had lunch in Corbridge—just as you said.'

Needless to say, Sara did not go to Linda's birthday party. She didn't know if Alex would have taken her in any case, but she didn't give him the chance to refuse. On the morning of the party she stayed in bed, complaining of a violent headache. And although she doubted whether Alex would believe her she actually felt as ill as she maintained.

She saw little of Alex in the days that followed. His mother said he'd had to make a business trip to London, but Sara had no illusions that he was avoiding her. And why not? she thought defensively. He must feel as bad about what had happened as she did. Or if not bad then at least guilty. He had betrayed his brother. That must mean something, even to him.

If his parents noticed the sudden chill that had developed between them when he returned they said nothing. They were too polite, Sara assumed. After all, they probably hadn't approved of their relationship in the first place.

She returned to London herself a little less than three weeks after that visit to Ragdale, and by then she already had her suspicions that all was not well. She should have started her period ten days ago, and although she told herself that it was excitement at the prospect of seeing Harry again the sentiments didn't quite ring true.

But what with preparing for the wedding—it was just to be a simple register office affair, with only close friends and family in attendance—and finishing her packing she succeeded in putting the problem out of her mind. It was made considerably easier at the news that Alex would not be coming to the wedding. He had had a lot of pain with his leg recently, his mother told Sara coldly. He hadn't rested it half enough in recent weeks, and he was paying the penalty now.

Of course, Sara didn't believe that. But happily Harry did, and the wedding itself went without a hitch. It was so good to see Harry again, to bask in his undemanding affection. He was the man she really loved, she told herself. That interlude with Alex had simply been summer madness, as he'd said.

But looked at now, from a distance of over five years, Sara's view seemed slightly flawed. Oh, she had loved Harry—she had no doubts about that. But after what had happened that afternoon at Ragdale she couldn't quite dismiss her feelings for Alex.

The truth was that ever since that evening at the apartment he had shared with Harry, when she'd assumed—erroneously, as it had turned out—that Alex had been attracted to her, she'd been rather too willing to believe the worst of him. The stories that Harry had told her—not quite what she had told Alex—had seemed to paint his brother in a dubious light, and she had seized on his evident popularity as a reason why she should despise him.

She had never once imagined that she might be jealous, that her willingness to exaggerate his faults had any personal connotation. The fact that Harry had seemed to enjoy her criticisms of his brother was just another example of her stupidity—and, perhaps, of a little sibling rivalry as well.

Sara sighed. Accusing Alex of telling Ben about his father's murder was just another example. The state she'd been in when she'd got back from Ragdale... She'd needed a scapegoat and he had been it. Besides, she needed to convince herself that Alex was as black as he'd been painted. If she had any doubts, her whole life might be proved a sham...

Christmas came and went without real incident.

To her relief, Ben said no more about how his father had died, though he did shed some tears on Christmas morning. It was when he discovered the bicycle that he'd been wanting among his presents. He remembered that Harry had promised to teach him to ride, and Sara spent some time assuring him that she could do it just as well.

But it was hard for Ben really to assimilate what had happened. He didn't truly understand why he wouldn't be seeing his father again. It was all very well telling herself that he knew Harry was dead, she realised. But to a four-year-old things were never that clean-cut.

They went to church on Christmas morning, and when they got back to the house Alex was there. As Sara hadn't seen him since the afternoon when she'd accompanied him and Ben to Ragdale, she greeted him rather stiffly, but Alex seemed unaware of her withdrawal.

Ben immediately decided that his uncle was better qualified to teach him how to ride his new bicycle than his mother, and Sara gave in gracefully when he put it to her. Besides, Alex said that he had a special present to show the boy, and they both went off together in good spirits.

It came as no real surprise to Sara when her son came dashing back some fifteen minutes later. For once even his grandmother didn't reprove him for charging into the room. He had something to show them, he said, begging his mother and his grandparents to come down to the stables. Uncle Alex's present was even more exciting than his bicycle.

It was a pony, of course. Even before Sara saw the pretty little Shetland, with its shaggy coat and soft brown eyes, she knew. Despite everything she'd said, Alex had gone ahead and got one. Well, actions spoke louder than words, she told herself firmly, incapable of disappointing Ben by offering any reproof.

All the same, she did exchange one speaking look with her brother-in-law. They were going to have to have a reckoning—there was no doubt about that. Not on Christmas Day, Sara accepted, tight-lipped, but before she and Ben departed for London.

The opportunity came a few days after New Year.

Alex had spent the New Year celebrations with the Erskines. According to Mrs Reed, it was traditional that James Erskine gave a party on New Year's Eve, and in the normal course of events she and Robert would have joined them too. But in the circumstances they had chosen to decline, and although Alex had had his doubts too Linda would have been disappointed if none of them had attended.

I'll bet she would, Sara had thought, trying to be charitable but failing. The knowledge that her brother-in-law would be spending the evening with the other woman had been a source of some resentment. Despite her liking for James Erskine, whom she had met on a couple of occasions since the funeral, when he and his

wife had dined at Perry Edmunds, she hadn't been able
to forget that he was considerably older than his wife,
and that the way Linda treated Alex was as someone
who was much closer than a friend.

Of course, it was nothing to do with her how Alex or
Linda spent their time, she'd assured herself, but her
suspicions had still simmered just the same. It was never
too late, she'd thought, guessing that Linda shared that
opinion. And Alex was much more stable now, as his
resignation from the news agency had proved.

Consequently, she was in no mood to award Alex any
concessions when he came into the sitting room one
morning and found her making a list of what she would
need to take away with her. She'd decided, if the Reeds
agreed, to leave most of her and Ben's belongings at
Perry Edmunds. Until they found a place of their own
they'd stay at a small hotel.

The appearance of her brother-in-law at such a time
was not welcome. She would have preferred to pick the
time for any encounter and she was considering leaving
the room when he blocked her way. 'Can we talk?' he
asked, his face hot, his hair ruffled from working down
at the stables. As always he struck her as being disturbingly physical, and her nerves tightened accordingly.

'Well, I am rather busy,' she said, hurriedly getting
up from the couch. If she'd known that she might see
him, she'd have taken a little more care about what she
was wearing. The Lycra leggings were thin—and far too
revealing.

'Not that busy, I'm sure,' declared Alex, closing the
door firmly and leaning back against it. 'You've been
avoiding me for weeks. Did you think I wouldn't notice?'

Sara checked that her loose-necked sweater covered
her rear, and then crossed her arms protectively over her
body. 'I don't know what you mean,' she said. 'I wasn't
aware we had any association. Just because Ben thinks

the sun shines out of your—well, just because he thinks you're wonderful I don't have to endorse that view. I'm afraid I'm not so easily impressed.'

Alex sighed. 'Here we go again.'

'What do you mean?'

'Don't pretend you don't know.' His lips twisted. 'Is this your way of dealing with it? D'you think if you ignore it it'll go away?'

'What will go away?'

Sara was genuinely puzzled now, and Alex straightened his back impatiently. 'You, me, Ben!' he informed her, with a fulminating look. 'Sara, the boy's my son. Whether you like it or not we have to deal with it. Now, we can do it politely—or not. It's up to you.'

Sara held up her head. 'You really think you can say something like that and get away with it?' She swallowed. 'It's rubbish, and you know it. You don't have an atom of proof. For some—nefarious reason you've decided to punish me. Because of what happened, I suppose.' She hesitated. 'Did I tarnish your image of irresistibility or what?'

'Don't be so bloody stupid!' Alex came away from the door now, and although Sara determinedly stood her ground she was not unaware of the threat he represented. And not just to her physical health, she admitted uneasily. Where Alex was concerned, she didn't trust herself at all.

'What would you consider proof?' he asked at last, having apparently controlled whatever impulse had inspired his earlier lunge. He regarded her steadily, his dark face and lean body disturbingly familiar. In spite of his having lost weight, the black trousers he was wearing still fitted him like a glove.

'I—you don't have any proof,' she stammered quickly. She licked her lips. 'Will you please get out of my way? I've got...things I want to do.' She'd almost said 'packing' but thought better of it. There was no reason for him to know that she was leaving until her plans were made.

'Harry couldn't have any children,' said Alex inflexibly. 'He had mumps when he was an adolescent. He was sterile.'

Sara's breath caught in her throat. 'You're lying.'

'Ask my mother.'

'But—but—' Sara was desperate. 'Lots of men—youths—get mumps. It doesn't necessarily follow that they can't ever—'

'Harry knew he couldn't have children,' said Alex flatly. 'He had some tests done when his relationship with Linda looked as if it might become serious.'

'His relationship with Linda?' echoed Sara sickly. 'He didn't have a relationship with Linda.' And when Alex didn't answer her she added, 'He—he said it was his mother who'd wanted him to marry Linda. He wasn't interested in her himself.'

Alex shrugged. 'What can I say?'

Sara stared at him painfully. 'You can say it isn't true, that you're making the whole thing up. Harry wasn't involved with Linda. Why, he didn't even like her.'

'Is that what he said?'

'Well...' Harry hadn't actually said that, but it was the impression he'd given. 'It doesn't matter what he said. It was me he married. Me!'

'Don't I know it?' Alex's response was bitter.

'You're just saying this to get back at me!' she protested. 'God, I must have really hurt your pride!'

Alex took a weary breath. 'My pride has nothing to do with it,' he told her levelly. 'For God's sake, Harry was practically engaged to Linda. At least, he was until he found out he couldn't father a son.'

Sara wanted to cry—not in anguish, she told herself, but in anger. Alex was lying. She was almost sure of it.

He just wanted her to doubt Ben's parentage. She grimaced. As if she hadn't already done that for herself.

'I think you're sick,' she said now, choosing the most offensive reason she could think of for him to have devised such a story. 'Harry always envied you, but I think *you* were jealous of your brother!'

'Oh, Sara!' It was as if his own anger was being submerged by hers, and, although she sensed that he wanted to take her and shake her and convince her that what he said was true, weariness was overtaking him—that, and, perhaps, a latent sense of shame.

'You can't do this, Alex!' she exclaimed now, gaining strength from his apparent weakness. 'I know you love Ben, and I'm sure you wish you could be a father to him, but—'

'I *am* his father,' broke in Alex doggedly. 'Good God, Sara, what do I have to do? OK, you want it all? Hell, I'll give it to you. Harry sent you here before the wedding for me to screw!'

'*No!*'

It was the only word she could force past her lips, but she reinforced its message by vigorously shaking her head.

'No,' she said again, and then added faintly, 'I don't believe you. I was right—you are sick. Let me get out of here.'

'Wait.' When she would have cannoned past him, the frantic emotions she was feeling giving her a strength she'd not known she possessed, he stopped her. 'It wasn't like that between us, and you know it. What I did— what we both did, we did in love. I told Harry to screw himself, if you want the truth.'

'No.'

Once again the word spilled from her lips, her whole world shifting and turning on its axis. Harry couldn't have said that. She didn't believe him. It was all a horrible ploy to steal her son.

Alex gazed at her sombrely. 'I know you don't want to believe me,' he said, 'but it is true.'

'He was your brother,' protested Sara piteously, and Alex ran savage fingers through his hair.

'Do you think I don't know that?' he demanded. 'Do you think I haven't thought long and hard before telling you this? I didn't want to tell you. For God's sake, if you'd been reasonable I wouldn't have had to tell you. But for some reason you've decided I'm your enemy, and there wasn't much else I could do.'

Sara shook her head. 'It's crazy—'

'Is it?' Alex shrugged. 'Evidently Harry didn't think so.'

'But how could he know? How could he even think...?'

'That we might be attracted to one another?' asked Alex drily. 'Oh, he knew that already. That night in London, remember? He knew I was infatuated with you then.'

Sara gasped. 'But you already had a girlfriend!' she exclaimed.

'Had I?' Alex's dark brows arched. 'That's the first I've heard of it. Who was I supposed to be dating? I'd just got back from a trip to the States.'

Sara hesitated. 'Oh, this is ridiculous!' she exclaimed finally. 'There were always women in your life. This woman was a model. I saw her pictured with you in the paper.'

Alex's expression was sardonic now. 'You saw my picture in some newspaper and you immediately thought the woman beside me was my girlfriend?'

'Well, no. Not exactly.' Sara tried to think. 'Harry told me she was your girlfriend.' She coloured at the obvious connotation. 'He wouldn't have lied to me. He wouldn't.'

'Suit yourself.' Alex lifted his shoulders. 'But I have the right to defend myself. *I* know who and when I was dating someone, not you.'

Sara shifted uncertainly. 'In any case, what has that to do with anything?'

'You tell me.'

'You can't deny there have been women.' She licked her lips. 'And—and if Harry was mistaken on that occasion he wasn't mistaken on others.'

'OK.' Alex chose not to argue about it. 'But don't ask me to tell you my life story. I've never hurt anyone— except, perhaps, you.'

'Oh, you hurt me all right,' cried Sara unsteadily. 'And for some reason you're hurting me still. As if—as if Harry would ask you to—well, seduce me!' Her face contorted. 'I've never heard anything so awful in my life.'

Alex sighed. 'It wasn't quite like that.'

'I'll bet it wasn't.' Sara stiffened her spine. 'Tell me, Alex, how long has it taken you to come up with this idea? Cajoling me didn't work, and I wouldn't take your threats seriously. So now you've decided to blacken my husband's memory by implying he had something to do with how you behaved.'

'Dammit, he wouldn't have been your husband if I'd had anything to do with it,' snarled Alex harshly. 'After what happened d'you think I didn't tell him what I'd done?' He snatched a breath. 'But you know what? Harry said it didn't matter. He wouldn't let you go whatever I said.'

'You saw Harry? Before the wedding?'

'Of course I did.' Alex groaned. 'Where did you think I went? I was still on sick leave, remember?'

'Your mother said you'd gone to London,' said Sara
faintly, and Alex pulled a wry face.

'Well, I did. Initially,' he conceded grimly. 'You have
to fly out of Heathrow if you're *en route* to Kuwait.'

'You went to Kuwait!' Sara was stunned. 'Harry never
said.' Nor had he told her that Alex had told him what
had happened, she thought ominously. Oh, God, Alex
couldn't be telling the truth. She felt afraid.

'Well, he wouldn't,' said Alex wearily. 'That was when
he told me he'd expected it. He knew I'd be attracted
to you, and he used us both.'

'No!' Sara wouldn't listen to him. 'Harry loved me!'

'Oh, I'm sure he did.' Alex was sardonic. 'Particularly as you were carrying *his* son.'

'You're just saying this to excuse the way you treated
me,' declared Sara painfully. 'Can't you see that you
proved Harry was right by coming on to me? If—if Harry
forgave you, then you should have been grateful, It can't
have been easy for him. Can't you see?'

Alex raised his eyes heavenward. 'You don't get this,
do you? You've simply closed your mind to any explanation but the one you choose to believe. God knows,
I sometimes wondered if Harry ever loved you, or if he
didn't just do it all to humiliate me.'

'You're paranoid!'

Unable to take any more of this, Sara forced her way
past him, making for the door on legs that showed a
decided tendency to shake. She felt as if everything she'd
known and believed in was tumbling around her. Despite her defence of Harry she was losing hope.

'Don't go!'

His tortured plea reached her as she put her hand on
the handle of the door. There was such a wealth of feeling in his voice that for once she found herself unable
to go on.

'Ben's my son,' he added brokenly, moving behind her, so that she could feel the heat of his body at her back. He moved the neckline of her sweater aside and brushed her soft skin with his tongue. 'I never wanted to hurt you, Sara. Harry knew—you are the only woman I've ever loved.'

CHAPTER TWELVE

IT WAS April, six months since Harry had died, and Sara was visiting his solicitors for the first time.

It would be Easter next week. The mild spring meant that the parks were already full of blossom, and Sara had bought a huge bunch of tulips to brighten up her rather dismal room.

She was supposed to be spending the holiday weekend with her in-laws. And, for all that she had no enthusiasm for the visit, she thought she'd probably go. If it meant spending some time with her son she'd travel anywhere. She missed him so much that it was sometimes hard to get through the day.

But at least she had a job now to distract her. She was earning good money at the hospital in Fulham Road, and recording patients' records onto computer disk wasn't hard. Besides, the people she worked with in the office were friendly, and although she didn't talk about her circumstances she had had to tell them she was a widow.

The women were very supportive. If Sara had wanted to she could have had company almost every night. But, for all their kindness, she preferred her anonymity. She guessed they thought that she was still racked with grief.

And she was, in a way, thought Sara ruefully. Though somehow she could never remember Harry with quite the same regret. In spite of telling herself that she didn't believe all of Alex's story, she couldn't dismiss the fact that Harry had kept his brother's visit from her.

She'd checked on that, of course. Despite the passage of years there were still people she knew in Kuwait, and with some prompting they'd remembered that Harry's brother had visited him in the summer of that year. It was an example of Alex's fame going before him. He'd been well-known then for his reports from the Middle East, and everyone had wanted to meet him.

It had been enough, anyway, to force Sara to review the situation. No man capable of fathering his own child could have accepted what his brother had done without remorse and then never voiced the knowledge to her. Dear God, there were times when she wondered if she'd really known Harry at all.

It had also made her think about the years they'd spent together. For all she'd believed that they were happy, now she was not so sure. All the little things that at the time had seemed unimportant might have had a deeper meaning than she'd thought.

Not least had been Harry's persistent estrangement from his family—an estrangement that she'd been all too eager to foster for her own ends. But what if Harry's reasons had echoed her apprehensions? Hadn't he wanted to face his brother? Had that been it?

Whatever the true circumstances surrounding Ben's conception, Sara had realised that she didn't have the right to go on thwarting Alex's claim. Besides, after that moment in the sitting room at Ragdale when he'd kissed her she'd realised he'd go to any lengths to get his own way—even to the point of pretending to care about her, she thought painfully. He was prepared to take her too, if that was the only way to reach his son.

That was why she'd decided to leave—at once; without giving him another chance to make a fool of her. Whatever latent emotions his kiss had kindled were not—and never could be—important to her. All right, Harry might have known that Ben wasn't his son; she had to

accept that. But as for his arranging it that way... No.
She thought she'd never forgive Alex for saying that.

Of course, the hardest part had been leaving Ben
behind at Perry Edmunds. Though in all honesty she
had to admit that her son hadn't put up much oppo-
sition. What with his new pony, whom he'd christened
Merrylegs, and the undoubted freedom he enjoyed by
living in the country, he wasn't much interested in moving
to a big city. He couldn't understand why his mother
wanted to go.

And so long as she kept in constant touch, either by
phone or by letters, which Christine could read to him,
for the present he seemed reasonably content. Occasionally his grandfather brought him down to London
to visit her, and that was harder—for both of them. But
Robert had assured her that Ben's tears usually dried by
the time they reached the airport.

Of course, she mused, he would say that. Like his
son, Robert had never wanted her to take Ben away from
Perry Edmunds right from the very beginning. And for
all his tears Ben seemed happy living with his grandparents. Certainly he never stopped talking about the
things he'd done and the places he'd been all the time
they were together.

Naturally, his 'uncle' Alex figured strongly in all these
recitals—which was what she had expected, Sara told
herself when the pain of her son's absence started to
bite. It was only right Ben should spend some time with
his father. For some time now she'd accepted that Alex
deserved as much.

All the same, she couldn't help how she felt when Ben
told her that he and Christine had been visiting Ragdale.
Sara assured herself that the twinges she felt on those
occasions were only envy—of Christine's closeness to her
son, she averred, and nothing else. She wasn't jealous;

jealousy would imply a different emotion. It was just difficult sometimes to cope with, that was all.

Of Alex himself she heard little. Since that morning when everything had come to a head, she hadn't even laid eyes on him. She had made her plans, independent of him, and executed them. If he thought that he'd won—well, perhaps he had.

For the future she had no definite objective. After Easter Ben was to start attending the kindergarten in Corbridge, and until he was older that was probably the wisest course. She had to accept that Alex was owed some moral privileges. Until her life was more secure Ben was better off where he was.

Now she pushed open the swing-doors that led into the office building. Harry's solicitors, Kaye and Brockway, were on the seventh floor. When she'd been here before—with Harry—she hadn't felt half as apprehensive. But then, she'd had nothing on her conscience in those days. That was before she'd spent those weeks at Edmundsfield.

She wouldn't have been here now if they hadn't written to her. The letter had been redirected from Perry Edmunds over a week ago. After what Alex had told her she hadn't wanted anything more from the Reeds. She knew that Harry had made her his sole beneficiary, but she'd decided that whatever money there was could be invested for Ben.

Still, Mr Brockway had been quite adamant that he needed her signature, and he'd reminded her that there was still the codicil of Harry's will to deal with. At least this would be the final formality, she thought painfully. Perhaps then she could lay Harry's ghost to rest.

A receptionist asked her to wait while she advised Mr Brockway that his client had arrived, and Sara flicked through the pages of a magazine without really seeing anything. The glossy layouts, the designer clothes, the exotic perfumes meant nothing to her. She just wanted this to be over.

'Will you come through, Mrs Reed?'

The receptionist was back, and, drying her damp palms on the seams of her woollen trousers, Sara followed the rather angular woman into a large, dusty office.

'Ah, Mrs Reed.'

Harry's solicitor was in his early fifties—a man of middle height, whose enjoyment of the good life was evident in the rather bulbous stomach that overhung his belt. But his face was friendly and he was smiling, and Sara greeted him politely before taking a seat.

'At last,' he said, and Sara decided that that didn't require an answer. 'I suppose it is quite a trek from Northumberland at this time of year.'

'Yes.'

Sara decided not to enlighten him. Where she was living now was nothing to do with him. And after today there'd be few reasons why he should need to get in touch with her. He had her in-laws' address; that was enough.

'Is it very cold there at present?'

That was harder. 'Um—reasonably, I think,' she said, feeling her cheeks turn pink. And then, because it was simpler, she admitted, 'As a matter of fact I've been living in London for—for several weeks. I...thought it would be easier to get a job here.'

'A job?' Mr Brockway sounded surprised. 'Well, if you feel you need to contribute, of course. But I should tell you, Mrs Reed, your husband has left you very well provided for.' His lips twisted slightly, as if he found the subject rather distasteful. 'As well as his insurance there are several hundred thousand pounds.'

Sara gulped. 'You're not serious.'

'Oh, I am.' Mr Brockway pursed his lips now, and extracted what she assumed to be Harry's file from his in-tray. He flicked it open and appeared to study its contents. 'His dealings in the emerald trade yielded quite a substantial sum.'

'His dealings in the emerald trade?' Sara stared at him disbelievingly. 'Are you telling me that Harry worked for an emerald cartel? But he was a civil servant; he worked for the government; I'd have known if he'd changed his job.' She licked her parched lips. 'I don't understand.'

'Evidently not.' Mr Brockway looked a little more sympathetic now. 'And no, Mrs Reed, your husband didn't work for an emerald cartel. His dealings were—how shall I put it?—independent. Such a pity he didn't think of protecting himself.'

Sara was horrified. 'Are you implying that Harry was—was—smuggling emeralds?'

'Heavens, no.' Mr Brockway looked quite scandalised at the suggestion. 'What he did was—strictly—legal. All I'm saying is that the people he dealt with couldn't always be trusted.'

Sara blinked. 'What are you trying to say?' She swallowed. 'Do you think his—his murder—wasn't a mistake, after all?'

'Well, it's possible,' agreed the solicitor evasively. 'Mr Reed always knew he was living life—how do they say it—on the edge? It may be that he died protecting the diplomat. But it's equally true that he had enemies in that part of the world as well.'

Sara's shoulders sagged. 'I can't believe it.'

'Well—' Mr Brockway sounded almost reassuring '—I don't suppose it matters. The fact remains that you're quite a wealthy woman now. Mr Reed wanted to be sure that you and his son were adequately supported. Which is why we need to discuss your future plans...'

* * *

Sara left the solicitor's office feeling dazed. How could she have lived with Harry for so long and not known what was going on? She was unhappily aware that it made what Alex had told her more believable. If he could keep something like this from her, what else might he have done?

She looked down at the envelope that Mr Brockway had given her. Her name was written on the front in Harry's handwriting. It contained the codicil that Mr Brockway had told her about. But they hadn't discussed it. Apparently Harry had left instructions that she was to read it privately. Although obviously the solicitor was aware of what it contained, he had to respect Harry's wishes.

She took a taxi from Lincoln's Inn back to Hammersmith. When she'd told her boss at the hospital that she had to see a solicitor about her late husband's will, he'd given her the afternoon off. In consequence she had the driver take her home, to the tiny flatlet she was renting, deciding that for once she could afford to be extravagant.

Nevertheless, the idea of all that money disturbed her, even though it was tempting to think of what it could buy... A large apartment, a house—one that had a garden, with a paddock where Ben could keep his pony. God, they were rich!

And Alex...

But she didn't want to think about Alex now. It was hard enough living with the knowledge that she might never see him again. Or only on those occasions when Ben was present. She had to remember that their son was their only point of contact. The past was as dead as the man she'd thought she knew.

CHAPTER THIRTEEN

AN HOUR later Sara was still sitting at the scarred Formica table, staring at the piece of paper in her hands. She was still wearing the navy parka that she'd worn to go to the solicitors' office, still clutching the key she'd used to open the door.

She could have shed her coat before opening the envelope. She could have filled the kettle and put it on the stove, or turned on a couple of bars of the electric fire. But as soon as she'd got through the door she'd known an overwhelming impulse to read what Harry had added to his will, to find out why he'd considered it necessary that she should read his wishes alone.

The codicil wasn't long. Initially it stated, in terms that even an idiot could have understood, that he'd known all along that Ben wasn't his son. As Alex had told her, Harry had found out years ago that he couldn't have children. But he wanted Sara to know that he forgave her, and that he'd always regarded the child as his own.

At this point Sara had taken a moment to compose herself. It wasn't easy accepting that she had been wrong. Evidently Alex had known his brother better than she had. But the obvious connotations were immense.

She'd read on, expecting Harry to reveal how Alex had gone to Kuwait and he'd discovered that the child was his brother's. It can't have been easy, whatever he said, she'd thought painfully, and her trembling hand had caused the printed page to dance before her eyes.

But there was no mention that Alex had been to see him—no mention of Alex at all in that regard. If she hadn't known better, Sara might have thought that Harry hadn't known who Ben's father actually was. And, indeed, if Alex hadn't spoken to her she might have found consolation in that fact.

But she did know, and Harry had known, yet he'd chosen not to reveal the truth to her. Whatever Alex had said to him, he'd totally ignored it. There was no reference to her stay at Perry Edmunds at all.

The rest of the document was taken up with the arrangements that he'd made for her and Ben's future. There'd be money enough for them to live comfortably, whatever happened. And funds for Ben's education, too, should anything unforeseen happen to him. It was a curious thing to mention. It seemed that Harry hadn't been totally unprepared for his sudden death.

But it was the stipulation he made at the end of the document that left Sara feeling devastated—the apparently innocent recommendation about where she should choose to live. Harry had made it plain that if he should predecease his parents he would rather she didn't go to live in Northumberland. He'd heard that his brother had bought a house there, and he didn't want Alex interfering in his son's life.

And she might have agreed with him, thought Sara tersely now, folding the paper and stuffing it back into its envelope, if she'd gone to the solicitors' office as soon as she'd arrived in England, which she might have done. Of course, Harry could have had no idea that his parents would insist on him being buried at Edmundsfield, and he'd relied on her antipathy towards Alex to keep his brother at bay.

Besides, in the normal course of events Ben would have been an adult before either of his parents had died. And once she and Harry had been back living in England he might have discarded the addition to his will. She would probably have never heard about it, unless some latent sense of pride had got in his way.

Whatever, it seemed that however much he'd professed to love Ben he hadn't wanted to be thought a fool. He'd wanted her to know that he hadn't been duped by what she'd done. Yet conversely he'd prevented her from telling him the truth, and when Alex had tried to intervene he'd sent him away.

Sara got up now, feeling totally drained. Her mind was buzzing with the implications of what she had learned, and whichever way she turned Harry's machiavellian schemes seemed to baulk her. It was obvious now that Harry had known exactly what he was doing. Unfortunately, without his volition, fate had taken a hand.

She filled the kettle and set it on the stove, and then stared somewhat bleakly out of the window. It was not an inspiring view. The rooftops of the houses opposite blocked most of the light, and below in the street there was the constant noise of traffic. It was not somewhere she'd choose to bring up her son. But, the way she felt right now, she wished he were there.

She wouldn't let herself think about Alex. She wouldn't even let herself dream that there'd been any truth in his declaration. He'd wanted Ben, not her, and now he'd got him. Or, at least, he could see as much of him as he liked.

For herself, she could see no alteration in her present circumstances. Whether or not the stipulation that Harry had made in the codicil would stand up in a court of law wasn't important. Its only connection with her was the money, and quite honestly she felt that even that was tainted now.

She'd told Mr Brockway that she'd get back to him, and during the following week she rang and explained that she'd read the document, and that she was very sorry but she had no intention of removing Ben from his grandparents' house. He was very happy there, and until she could afford a home that would suit them both she had decided to leave him where he was.

'But what about the money, Mrs Reed?' Mr Brockway couldn't believe that she intended to ignore such an enormous sum.

'If it can't be invested until Ben's older, give it to charity,' replied Sara tersely. 'And that goes for Harry's insurance too. I prefer to support myself.'

The solicitor hummed and hawed, but eventually he was obliged to accept that Sara meant what she'd said. He promised he'd investigate the legitimacy of Harry's instructions and get back to her. But Sara told him not to hurry. She had everything she needed.

She decided not to go to the Reeds' for Easter, after all. Somehow, after the traumatic events of the past week, she didn't think that she could face Alex just yet. She was very much afraid that if she did she might break down in front of him. He was not the man she'd thought he was, and she needed time to recover her self-respect.

And her self-control, she realised ruefully, aware of the barriers that her new knowledge had torn down. She'd spent the past five years reviling him for seducing her, when now she knew that she had been equally to blame.

She missed Ben horribly, so she spent the holiday weekend spring-cleaning her tiny apartment, only going out on Sunday morning to the nearby church. She loved the church at Easter, when it was decked out with all the spring blossoms. And the service was so joyful that she couldn't help feeling better when it was over.

Then, approximately three weeks later, she got a call from James Erskine.

When the landlady came up the stairs that evening to tell her that she was wanted on the phone, Sara immediately thought that something must have happened to Ben. She hadn't spoken to him for a few days, and Christine hadn't replied to her last letter. Dear God, she thought as she hurried down the stairs, please don't let anything have happened to him. He was the only person who gave her his unconditional love.

Hearing James's voice gave her a decided start, and she wondered apprehensively if her fears had been misplaced. But if either Robert or Elizabeth Reed was ill surely Alex would have told her? Just because they were barely on speaking terms there was no reason why he wouldn't keep her informed.

However, James assured her that both Ben and her in-laws were in the best of health. 'Linda had Christine bring Ben over to swim in the pool just the other afternoon,' he declared, unwittingly causing Sara to grit her teeth. 'He's a grand little boy. You have every reason to be proud of him.'

'Thank you.'

Sara managed to sound reasonably civil, even though the thought of Linda Erskine influencing her son was hard to bear. Had Alex been there as well? she wondered bitterly. It was a question she had no right to ask.

'Anyway,' James went on, apparently noticing nothing amiss, 'as I'm staying in London for a couple of nights, I wondered if we might have dinner one evening. Tomorrow evening, if that's convenient. I'm staying at the Grosvenor Hotel, and there's a rather charming Italian restaurant not far from there.'

'Oh, I...'

Sara wanted to refuse but she didn't know how. The last thing she needed was an evening with James and Linda Erskine. She could just imagine the mileage that the other woman would make from her absence, particularly as she saw Ben more frequently than his own mother.

'I'd appreciate it if you would,' James persisted, sensing a refusal. 'I'm on my own, you see, and I hate dining alone. We could make it fairly early—half past seven or eight if you'd prefer it. I realise you have a job and you won't want to be late.'

Sara's shoulders sagged. He was on his own! That put an entirely different complexion on it. Though when she thought about it she should have just as many misgivings. After all, why would he seek her out? They were hardly friends.

But however deplorable it might be the idea of hearing about Alex, even second-hand, was an irresistible attraction. When she spoke to Ben, and in her letters, she consciously had to avoid asking any overt questions. Ben talked about him, of course, but always in reference to what *he* had been doing. James knew Alex socially; it would be acceptable to ask how Alex was.

The following evening she arrived at the restaurant before he did. But he'd booked a table, and she was shown immediately to it instead of having to wait. She spent the time studying the other diners and comparing what they were wearing. At least her ankle-length pinafore-dress wasn't out of place.

The waiter came and asked if she would like a drink, and she ordered a martini. She had intended just to drink wine, but she felt as if she needed a boost. Despite assuring herself that she had nothing to fear from James Erskine, she was still nervous. She wasn't totally convinced that Linda wasn't with him after all.

She was sipping her martini and studying the enormous menu that the waiter had handed her when a shadow swept over the table. At last, she thought with some relief, lifting her head. But it wasn't Linda's elderly husband who was standing in front of her. It was Alex, and the glass slipped from her nerveless fingers.

'Can I sit down?' he asked as a waiter hurried over to attend to the spillage, and Sara could only nod. 'We'll have another two of those,' he added, addressing the young Italian. And then, pulling out a chair, he seated himself beside her.

He looked very pale, she thought, trying to be objective. It was as if all the natural colour had been drained out of his face. And there were bags beneath his eyes, and his face had a curious air of dissipation—as if he'd been on a terrific bender and he'd just come round.

'I—are you...? That is, James—'

'He won't be coming,' said Alex flatly, lifting the drink that the waiter had brought for him and swallowing at least half its contents at a single gulp. 'I'm sorry. I hope you'll forgive my small deception. I was afraid if I asked you myself you wouldn't come.'

Sara swallowed. 'Is James—I mean—are the Erskines here in London?' she asked, as if it mattered to her.

'James is,' conceded Alex wryly. 'But he's dining at his club, so he won't be joining us.' His lips twisted. 'I heard what he said to you yesterday evening, but he won't be lonely. I congratulated him on his ingenuity. I couldn't have handled it better myself.'

Sara looked down at the drink that had replaced the one she'd dropped, and wondered if she could lift it without having another mishap. Her whole body felt strangely nerveless now, and she had no wish to embarrass herself again.

Deciding that she had to take the risk, she wrapped both hands round the glass and brought it carefully to her lips. The gin was marvellously reviving. After a few sips she was almost capable of looking at him without her emotions glowing in her eyes.

'Don't you want to know why I'm here?' asked Alex at last, when it became apparent that Sara wasn't about to ask him. 'Or is my appearance such an aberration? I'm sorry, but I felt we needed to talk.'

'Here?' said Sara faintly, not at all sure that she wanted to hear what he might have to say to her. She was far too aware of the pain of their last meeting. She couldn't believe that what he had to say might be anything good.

'It seemed neutral enough,' he replied, emptying his glass. He summoned the waiter to order another and then leaned back in his chair. 'I don't want you walking out on me this time.'

'I didn't walk out on you.'

'Didn't you?' Alex arched a quizzical brow. 'As I recall it, you couldn't wait to get away from me the last time. What is it about my feelings that gives you a hard time?'

Sara's lips parted. 'I—don't know what you mean,' she protested, using her glass as a kind of shield. She buried her nose in it nervously. This was not the way she had expected their conversation to go.

'Sure you do,' he said flatly. 'Thanks.' This was directed at the waiter who had delivered his second drink. He took a mouthful of the clear liquid and savoured it. 'Were you like that with Harry, or is it only me?'

The colour in Sara's cheeks deepened. 'Like what?' she asked, aware that the question didn't really deserve an answer. 'I don't know what you're talking about.' She took a breath. 'How's Ben? It seems ages since I've seen him.'

Alex swallowed another measure of his martini. At this rate he'd be onto his third before they'd decided what they were going to eat, thought Sara uneasily. And Alex intoxicated was not a desirable prospect. He was hard enough to handle when he was sober.

'It is ages,' he agreed, and to her relief he put his glass back on the table. 'He was expecting you to come home for Easter. We all were. But...you didn't choose to show.'

'It didn't seem worth it,' said Sara hurriedly, glancing unseeingly round the restaurant.

'Why not?'

'Well...because it didn't. It's a long way to go for just a weekend.'

'You didn't consider that I might wish to see you?' he asked pointedly. 'As you appear to have accepted that I'm Ben's father, don't you think you owe me an explanation?'

'Perhaps.' Sara expelled her breath on a long sigh. 'But...it isn't easy for me—'

'Do you think it's easy for me?' he interrupted her harshly, his voice rising. 'Because let me tell you it isn't. It's not easy at all. It's bloody hard—particularly when the other person involved won't even speak to you. For God's sake, Sara, can't you give me a break?'

'Keep your voice down!' exclaimed Sara apprehensively, aware that they were attracting attention. 'I don't know what more you want from me. I've practically given you my son. All right, he's your son too—I accept that. But short of telling him you're his father...' She shook her head.

'This is not about Ben,' said Alex wearily, resorted to another gulp of his martini. 'Believe it or not, I'm very grateful for what you've done. But knowing Ben was only half of the equation.' He heaved a sigh. 'I guess I only used him to get to you.'

CHAPTER FOURTEEN

'ARE you ready to order now, sir?'

The waiter at Alex's elbow forced him to drag his gaze from Sara's stunned face. And while he made some excuse about them not having decided yet she took the time to regain her composure.

He didn't mean it!

That was her first—and instinctive—reaction. For some reason he felt it was necessary to pretend that there was some emotional bond between them. Perhaps the more he got to know Ben, the deeper the attachment he felt towards him, and because of that he wanted to believe that the child had been conceived not in lust but in love.

The waiter went away again, and Sara wondered if only she was aware of the portentousness of the silence that had fallen. But, dear Lord, she thought, how was she supposed to answer him? She was afraid that her own feelings were too fragile to be discreet.

'Well?' said Alex at last, rather cynically. 'Aren't you going to tell me it serves me right? What's that old adage about playing with fire? I guess I deserved to get my hands burned, hmm?'

Sara took a deep breath. 'Look,' she said carefully, 'there's no need to do this—'

'To do what?' Alex was staring at her with wary eyes.

'To—pretend you—had some feelings for me.' Sara licked her lips. 'There's no reason why—why we can't be friends.'

'Friends?' Alex sucked in a gulp of air convulsively. 'Sara, I didn't come here to ask for your friendship.' His lips twisted. 'If this doesn't work out, I won't be around.'

Sara caught her breath. 'No!' Now her hands moved agitatedly across the table, almost knocking over the narrow flute of pink carnations that formed a centrepiece on the matching cloth. 'No, you can't think of— Alex, that's crazy! Ben—Ben needs you. He needs you in his life.'

'But you don't,' said Alex flatly, making no attempt to take hold of her reaching hands. 'And don't worry; I'm not thinking of committing suicide. I just meant I'm thinking of taking a job in the States.'

Sara slumped, sagging back in her chair and staring at him disbelievingly. 'But—but what about Ragdale? You said—you said you'd decided to give up journalism.' She hesitated. 'What about Ben?'

'Yeah, what about Ben?' he said, rubbing his forehead tiredly. 'I guess you get to keep him after all.'

Sara couldn't take this in. 'You're saying—you don't want him now?'

'No.' Alex's response was harsh. 'For God's sake, Sara, what do you think I am—a robot?'

'Then—'

'I'm saying I can't go on living at Ragdale without you. When you didn't turn up at Easter I knew I'd lost.'

'Lost?'

'Lost you!' he said thickly. 'Dammit, Sara, how many ways do I have to say this? I wanted you six years ago and I want you now. But—hell, you don't even care that I exist!'

'That's not true.' Sara quivered.

'No. Right. You're too sensitive to wish I was dead, but you don't really like me. I should have known I was wrong from the beginning. What was I? Just a bit of extramarital sex?'

'No.' Sara was horrified. 'It wasn't like that.'

'What was it like, then? Tell me.' He propped his elbows on the table. 'Was it good?'

Sara's face flamed, but she knew that she had to answer him. 'I think you know the answer to that for yourself.'

Alex's eyes darkened. 'So why did you act like I'd assaulted you? Why did you treat me like a leper from then on?' He hesitated. 'You know, when I went to see Harry I hoped—*prayed*—that he'd beat me up, just so long as he cancelled the wedding. The thought of you marrying anyone else was—torture!'

Sara stared at him. 'That can't be true.'

'Why can't it?' His expression was weary. 'I knew there was no point in appealing to you. You'd got this picture of me as some kind of macho stud firmly fixed in your head, and what happened—well, I guess it only reinforced that image in your mind. In any case, you didn't want to hear any explanations from me. You were set and determined to marry my brother, and that was that.'

Sara's tongue moistened her upper lip. 'And Harry didn't beat you up?'

'Hell, no!' Alex was savage. 'That was when I realised I'd played into his hands. He said that for the first time he'd got something I wanted and nothing I did was going to alter that.'

Sara shook her head. 'It's unbelievable.'

'To you, maybe.'

'No.' She paused. 'I mean I find it unbelievable that you should—should want me, as well as Ben. I always thought he was your only objective.'

Alex flung himself back in his chair. 'So now you know the truth. It's a good laugh, isn't it?' He glanced around. 'D'you want to order?'

'Do you?'

'Me?' He gazed at her warily. 'Oh, no. Don't tell me you want to end this meeting right now.'

'No.' Sara paused again. 'Well, here, perhaps. I'm—I'm really not very hungry, not for a proper meal. You—you can come back to my place, if you like. I could make us an omelette instead.'

Alex finished his drink. 'Is there any point?'

'I think so.' Sara put her drink aside.

'So that you can comfort me with an omelette, instead of apples?' he enquired mockingly. 'Is that what you have in mind?'

'Not exactly.' Sara folded her napkin. 'I—I agree with you, actually. I think we do need to talk. You see—' she hesitated '—I always believed you hated me, too.'

Alex stared at her. 'Why would you think a thing like that?'

'Oh, come on.' Sara crumpled the edge of the napkin between her fingers. 'After—after what happened, you didn't exactly behave as if—well, as if it was planned.'

'Because it wasn't.' Alex regarded her intently now. 'God, I didn't take you to Ragdale to make love to you. If I'd been thinking clearly I'd never have laid a hand on you at all. I'd realised by that time that I was falling in love with you. What I should have done was tell you how I felt.'

Sara gazed at him. 'So why didn't you?'

'I intended to—when the right moment came along. But that morning at Ragdale you were so sweet—so sexy. I guess you could say I simply lost my head.'

Sara swallowed. 'And afterwards?'

'Afterwards?' Alex gave her an old-fashioned look. 'You have to be joking. You practically tore my head off when I asked you how you felt. I have *some* pride, and you did your best to destroy it. There were times during that journey to Kuwait when I doubted I was quite sane.'

'Oh, Alex.' Sara caught her breath. 'I thought I was just another of your conquests. And I was so ashamed. I was engaged to Harry, after all.'

'Yeah.' Alex's mouth curled. 'So you told me. In no uncertain terms, if I remember correctly.'

'Yet—yet you still went to see Harry.'

'Oh, sure. I was convinced that what I was doing was right. I'd told myself that, given time, you'd thank me for being honest. But—well, it didn't quite work out as I had planned.'

Sara moistened her lips. 'Because of Harry.'

'Partly. But after I got back I began to have my doubts. You—well, you simply avoided me. That's the kindest way to put it. And I convinced myself you deserved everything you got.'

'I'm sorry...'

'You're sorry?' He looked taken aback. 'For what? For making love with me? For Harry's intransigence? For ruining my life?'

'For wasting so much time,' whispered Sara softly. 'If you'll come home with me, I'll show you what I mean.'

She looked round for the waiter then, but before she could catch the man's eye Alex grabbed her hands. 'Are you saying what I think you're saying?' he demanded harshly. 'Aw—hell, Sara, let's get out of here. At once.'

While Alex dealt with the perplexed waiter Sara collected her coat, and then they stepped out into the cool air of a May evening. Above the odour of diesel, Sara thought she could smell orange-blossom. But perhaps it was just the intoxication of her senses.

They took a taxi back to Hammersmith, and although Alex held her hand in the cab he made no attempt to kiss her. He didn't have to, she thought breathlessly, aware of his eyes caressing her in the muted light from the streetlamps. It was as if he didn't dare take his eyes away from her, as if he was afraid that she was some mirage that might disappear if he wasn't vigilant, and by the time the cab stopped in Honiton Street Sara felt as if every inch of her skin was burning.

'My landlady said I—I'm not supposed to have male visitors here after ten o'clock,' Sara ventured as they climbed the stairs, and Alex made a sound of wry amusement.

'Tough,' he said as she fumbled for her key. 'I guess she'll have to throw me out, then, because I'm not leaving.'

Sara's lips trembled. 'No?'

He looked down at her. 'Well, am I?'

'No,' she confessed huskily, and then, finally finding the lock, she pushed the door open.

He barely gave her time to turn on the light. As soon as the door was closed he propelled her back against it and covered her lips with his.

Her incredible recognition of his mouth staggered her. She had believed the past was behind her, but it wasn't. It was here and now, and when his tongue slid between her teeth she was instantly transported back to the hot, dusty little room at Ragdale, where she had known such unforgettable passion.

Alex's hands were on her, and every touch of his lips, every brush of his lean body, every scent and smell and taste of him was unbearably familiar. It was as if he had imprinted his image on her, just as surely as she had imprinted hers on him, and she had the feeling that the rest of her life had just been a prologue to this moment, to this man; to this love that she had denied for so many barren years.

With a little cry she wound her arms around his neck, and although he had been holding himself away from her now he slumped against her. His hard body crushed hers against the door, and his kiss deepened to a hungry demand.

'Not here,' he groaned, forcing himself up on his hands, and for the first time she became aware of the shabbiness of the room. It had been her home for so many weeks that she had forgotten how it must look to someone used to the comforts of Ragdale or Perry Edmunds. Even the pretty rug that she had thrown over the divan to make it look more like the couch it served as during the day couldn't hide its cheapness, and beyond the partition the electric heater gurgled off-puttingly.

'I—I'm sorry,' she said, aware that she was still wearing her coat, even if Alex had torn it open so that he could touch her tender breasts through her dress. 'I shouldn't have brought you here. But I've got used to it, and—'

Alex's hand gripping her jaw silenced her. 'What the hell are you talking about?' he demanded, and then bent his head to bite her lips, as if even now he couldn't get enough of her. 'I'm not going anywhere else.'

'But I thought . . .' Sara's lips were tingling from his urgent caress. 'You said—'

'What I meant was I'd rather not do it here, standing up, with all our clothes on,' Alex exhorted huskily. 'For heaven's sake, Sara, do you really think I care where we are so long as we're together?'

Sara trembled. 'Then—'

'Oh, come here.' Losing patience, Alex pulled her against him, parting his legs so that she could rest intimately against him. 'Does that feel as if I'm in any state to go back to my hotel?' he demanded half-angrily. 'God, Sara, I'm afraid this is going to be the fastest mating on record!'

Then, swinging her up into his arms, he carried her to the divan. While she thrust off her coat he divested himself of his own shirt and jacket, but when his fingers went to the buckle of his belt Sara stopped him. 'Let me,' she said, kneeling up, and he peeled the straps of her pinafore-dress from her shoulders as she unbuckled his belt and drew down the zip.

Beneath his dark trousers his arousal swelled provocatively against the thin cotton of his shorts, and her fingers trembled as she invaded that wholly masculine domain. His swiftly indrawn breath made her wonder if she was hurting him, but his expression was entirely sensual as he bore her back against the coverlet.

'I'm sorry,' he said, his hand sliding beneath the hem of her skirt and moving swiftly over her silk-covered inner thigh to the sweating junction of her legs. For the first time she wished she'd worn stockings instead of the all-encompassing tights, but his fingers moved up to slip beneath the waistband of both the tights and her panties. 'Let me do this,' he said unsteadily, tugging the offending garments down her legs, and then, with them pooled about her ankles, he parted her thighs and moved between them. 'Forgive me,' he said as he thrust his throbbing erection into her tight, moist core, and because she was incapable of speaking at that moment Sara let her body answer for her.

It was over fairly quickly, as he'd promised, but Sara had been brought to such a state of arousal by his hungry mouth that when he uttered a hoarse cry and spilled his seed inside her his flooding warmth sent her careering over the edge. The pulsing heat of his body seemed to match the violent beating of her heart, and it was only when he moved that she realised his heart was beating just as fast.

'Sorry,' he said again, against her mouth this time, and she lifted her hand to touch his hot face.

'For what?' she asked huskily. And then, knowing the answer for herself, but needing to hear him say it anyway, she asked, 'Wasn't it good?'

Alex lifted himself on his elbows to look down at her. 'For me?' he asked. 'Oh, yes. I've never had such hot sex before.'

'Hot sex?' Sara faltered. 'But I thought...'

'You thought?' he prompted, his eyes mocking her. 'What did you think, I wonder? That you'd make me say how good it was? That you saved my life? That I'm so crazy about you, I couldn't even wait to take your clothes off?'

Sara swallowed. 'Well,' she said uneasily, 'something like that.'

Alex relented. 'Or would you prefer the truth, hmm?' And, at the anxious darkening of her eyes, he said, 'It was incredible, yes. But then, it was nothing less than I expected. When you care for someone as much as I care for you, it couldn't be anything else.'

Sara's face cleared. 'Do you mean that?'

'Yes, I mean it,' he said, rolling onto his side and starting to remove her panties and tights from her ankles. Then, having disposed of them, he tackled the rest of her clothes, which were presently balled about her waist. 'And when you're good and naked I'm going to prove it to you,' he added, bending to press his face against her quivering stomach. 'How does that sound?'

It sounded pretty good to Sara, and he was as good as his word. She had never imagined that her little bed would ever hold such delights, but Alex was endlessly intuitive. With his hands and his lips and his tongue he taught her all there was to know about her own sexuality. She'd never imagined that she could be so responsive in so many different places, and she lost count of the times she lost herself in the hungry possession of his mouth.

He made love to her in so many different ways. From the teasing stroking of his tongue against the sole of her foot to the gentle abrasion of his teeth as he sucked her nipples. He kissed every inch of her—her neck, her shoulders, the silky curve of her inner thigh. He even explored her wrists and ankles, and the amazingly sensitive backs of her knees.

Once he had her straddle him, and she felt the throbbing length of him filling her completely. He taught her how to move with him and the image of herself, with her head thrown back, controlling his bucking body, was one she would always cherish.

But ultimately it was when he made love to her that she lost all her inhibitions. With her nails digging into his shoulders she let herself go where she had never gone before, and the dizzying heights of her fulfilment left her floating mindlessly in space...

Hours later she opened her eyes to a dazzling new dawn. It had been almost morning when they'd fallen asleep, and now she blinked at the clock on her bedside table with disbelieving eyes. If she wasn't mistaken it was already almost noon, and any thought of turning up for work that day was going to have to be abandoned.

She rolled onto her back as the recollection of the night before swept over her, but if she'd expected to encounter Alex's warm body she was disappointed. She was alone in the bed, and the realisation that this had happened to her before brought a chilling hollowing to her stomach. Dear God! Surely he hadn't left her?

And then she heard something behind her. It was probably the sound that had awakened her, she realised, turning over and peering across the room. Her heart and stomach turned over at the sight of Alex pouring water into her earthenware teapot, and the sight of the two mugs residing on the tray beside him explained his activity. But it was the fact that he was making the tea stark naked that caused the sudden gulp of laughter to escape her lips.

He swung round at the sound, and she saw at once that he was by no means indifferent to her appraisal. 'Did I disturb you?' he asked, putting the teapot on the tray and carrying it across to the bed. 'I dropped the damn teacaddy.'

'You always disturb me,' she admitted huskily, and Alex abandoned the tray on the bedside table and came urgently down beside her.

'Likewise,' he breathed, tossing the covers aside. And at her protest that she was cold he uttered a very satisfied groan. 'I'll warm you,' he said, nudging her thighs apart. 'Is this better?'

It was some time later that he remembered the tea, and as Sara sat demurely sipping the now rather cool beverage Alex squatted cross-legged beside her. 'We never did get to talk,' she murmured ruefully. 'And what is my boss going to say when I tell him I won't be turning up for work today?'

Alex's mouth compressed. 'If I have my way, you won't be turning up for work at all,' he replied softly 'You are going to put me out of my misery, aren't you?'

Sara dimpled. 'I thought I already had.'

'Not nearly.' Alex sobered. 'I want you to marry me, Sara. Will you?'

Despite everything that had gone before, Sara's cheeks reddened. 'Oh, Alex.'

'Is that a yes or a no?' he asked huskily, and she thrust her cup aside and launched herself into his arms.

'It's a yes,' she said half-tearfully. 'Oh, Alex, I do love you.'

'I should hope so,' he said rather smugly. And then with rather less composure he added, 'Does this mean you forgive me about—well, about what happened with Harry?'

'There's nothing to forgive,' Sara protested, and, resting her head on his shoulder, she explained what had happened at the solicitors.

'Damn!' Alex was incredulous. 'So the—so he always intended to keep us apart?'

'It seems like it.'

'And it would have happened that way if you hadn't come back to Perry Edmunds and I hadn't realised that I couldn't live without you, after all.'

'And seen Ben,' Sara reminded him gently, and Alex nodded.

'My son,' he said, a little emotionally. 'God, what do you think he's going to say about—well, about this?'

'I should think he'll be highly delighted,' murmured Sara wryly. 'You know what he thinks about you. Ever since you met you've been his hero.'

'Do you think so?'

Sara gave him a wry look. 'Don't you?'

Alex shook his head. 'I just wanted to hear you say it.'

Sara laughed. 'Oh, love—he'll be positively ecstatic. Besides,' she added, dimpling again, 'I never wanted just one child, and now—'

'Now we'll have another.'

'At least,' she conceded. 'I think four is a nice number, don't you?'

Alex laughed now. 'Whatever you say. It's just as well we've got a big house. It looks like we're going to need it.'

'Mmm.' Sara made a contented sound. 'So...' She looked at him a little anxiously. 'You won't be going to work in the States, will you?'

'Not now,' he agreed. 'As a matter of fact, I've been offered the chance to work for the local legal aid society, but I knew I couldn't stay around if we weren't together. It would have been too painful.'

'Would it?'

Sara kissed him lingeringly, and he caught his breath. 'You'd better believe it. And—by the way—I didn't tell Ben about—well, about Harry's murder. Someone called Conchita did.'

'Conchita?' Sara stared at him. 'She was one of the servants Harry employed in Rio.'

'Well, apparently he heard her and someone else talking about the murder. They said Harry had been shot, and, although Ben didn't really understand what that meant, when Linda started talking about killing foxes he suddenly got the connection. Thankfully, I think he's forgotten all about it again, but when he's older we'll get around to explaining it to him.'

'You won't...'

'Tell him that the bullet might have been for Harry, after all? No.' Alex heaved a sigh. 'I guess I can be that generous.'

'And the other?'

'The fact that I'm his father?' Alex shrugged. 'I guess that can wait too. When he's older he may understand. If not—well, hopefully by then he'll have a brother or sister who can explain it to him. He's a very pragmatic little boy. He'll be OK.'

'I'm sure.' Sara sighed. 'Your mother's not going to like this, though.'

'You think not?'

'Well, she never liked me, did she?'

'She was—wary of you.' Alex grimaced. 'I sometimes wonder if she had some idea of what Harry was doing by sending you to stay at Perry Edmunds as he did. She never admitted to knowing that Harry couldn't have any children, but she must have done. We'll probably never know.'

'Well, she seemed to encourage us to spend time together,' conceded Sara thoughtfully, and Alex made an impatient sound.

'Yeah, I know. But you have to remember she was still nurturing hopes of Harry changing his mind and marrying Linda. Maybe she thought if she pushed us together...'

'I'd break my engagement to Harry?'

Alex lifted his shoulders. 'It's possible. It's equally possible that she—like Harry—wanted a grandchild at any cost.'

'Oh, Alex.' Sara snuggled closer to him. 'If only I hadn't been such an idiot!'

'I'll second that,' he said softly. 'You've no idea how I felt when you insisted you loved Harry. I thought I loved my brother, but I was as jealous as hell then.'

'Unfortunately I think Harry was jealous of you,' said Sara thoughtfully. 'Poor Harry! I can feel sorry for him now.'

'And me,' agreed Alex ruefully. 'But I have to wonder when he decided to marry you. Was it before or after he saw us together?'

'Who knows?' Sara sighed, and then, determinedly introducing a light note, said, 'I was jealous too, you know—first of that model in London, then Linda—which reminds me, what was Karen Summers doing at your house?'

Alex laughed again. 'Well, she wasn't helping me choose the decorations,' he assured her gently. 'No, I interviewed her once for the agency, and when she was appearing in Newcastle afterwards she called me up and invited herself to dinner.'

'And that's all?' Sara stared at him.

'Honestly.' He sobered. 'I wouldn't lie to you, sweetheart. Not for anything. Do you believe me?'

'I do now,' she confessed huskily. 'Oh, I can't believe all this is happening. I'm sure it's just a dream.'

'Then let me convince you,' he said, tipping her onto her back and covering her with his body. 'We've got the rest of our lives to get it right...'

by
Miranda Lee

Complete stories of love down under that
you'll treasure forever.

Watch for:

#1855 *A WEEKEND TO REMEMBER*

It was only a little white lie...but before she knew it,
Hannah had pretended she was Jack Marshall's fiancée.
How long would it be before Jack regained his memory?

Available in December wherever
Harlequin books are sold.

ATR1

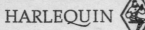

HARLEQUIN PRESENTS®

MEMO

To: The Reader

From: The Editor at Harlequin Presents

Subject: #1853 MISTLETOE MAN

by Kathleen O'Brien

Three years ago Daniel Blaisdell fired Lindsay
because she dared suggest there was more to life
than business—like falling in love. Now Lindsay
has a major deal to negotiate with her ex-boss....

P.S. Harlequin Presents—the best has just
gotten better! Available in December
wherever Harlequin books are sold.

P.P.S. Look us up on-line at: http://www.romance.net

NINE6

If you are looking for more titles by

ANNE MATHER

Don't miss these fabulous stories by one of
Harlequin's most distinguished authors:

Harlequin Presents®

#11492	BETRAYED	$2.89	☐
#11542	GUILTY	$2.89	☐
#11553	DANGEROUS SANCTUARY	$2.89	☐
#11591	TIDEWATER SEDUCTION	$2.99	☐
#11663	A SECRET REBELLION	$2.99 U.S.	☐
		$3.50 CAN.	☐
#11697	STRANGE INTIMACY	$2.99 U.S.	☐
		$3.50 CAN.	☐
#11731	RAW SILK	$3.25 U.S.	☐
		$3.75 CAN.	☐
#11759	TREACHEROUS LONGINGS	$3.25 U.S.	☐
		$3.75 CAN.	☐

(limited quantities available on certain titles)

TOTAL AMOUNT	$	
POSTAGE & HANDLING	$	
($1.00 for one book, 50¢ for each additional)		
APPLICABLE TAXES*	$	
TOTAL PAYABLE	$	

(check or money order—please do not send cash)

To order, complete this form and send it, along with a check or money order
for the total above, payable to Harlequin Books, to: **In the U.S.:** 3010 Walden
Avenue, P.O. Box 9047, Buffalo, NY 14269-9047; **In Canada:** P.O. Box 613,
Fort Erie, Ontario, L2A 5X3.

Name: _____

Address: _____ City: _____

State/Prov.: _____ Zip/Postal Code: _____

*New York residents remit applicable sales taxes.
Canadian residents remit applicable GST and provincial taxes.   HAMBACK6

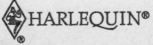

Look us up on-line at: http://www.romance.net

HARLEQUIN PRESENTS®

by Charlotte Lamb

Coming next month:

#1852 HOT BLOOD

Kit and Liam were business partners by day and lovers
by night. Without warning, tensions erupted between
them—and Kit found that, beneath his calm, controlled
exterior, Liam was red-hot!

Love can conquer the deadliest of Sins.

Available in December wherever
Harlequin books are sold.

SINS7